THE PSYCHIC TRAP

THE PSYCHIC TRAP

John Newton Chance

Chivers Press   •   G.K. Hall & Co.
Bath, England   Thorndike, Maine USA

This Large Print edition is published by Chivers Press, England, and by G.K. Hall & Co., USA.

Published in 2001 in the U.K. by arrangement with Robert Hale Limited.

Published in 2001 in the U.S. by arrangement with Robert Hale Limited.

U.K. Hardcover   ISBN 0-7540-4481-5   (Chivers Large Print)
U.K. Softcover   ISBN 0-7540-4482-3   (Camden Large Print)
U.S. Softcover   ISBN 0-7838-9445-7   (Nightingale Series Edition)

The text of this Large Print edition is unabridged.
Other aspects of the book may vary from the original edition.

Set in 16 pt. New Times Roman.

Printed in Great Britain on acid-free paper.

British Library Cataloguing in Publication Data available

Library of Congress Cataloging-in-Publication Data

Chance, John Newton.
    The psychic trap / John Newton Chance.
      p. cm.
    ISBN 0-7838-9445-7 (lg. print : sc : alk. paper)
    1. Art thefts—Fiction. 2. Country homes—Fiction.
    3. Seances—Fiction. 4. England—Fiction. 5. Large type books.
    I. Title.
PR6005.H28 P79 2001
823'.912—dc21   2001016736

CHAPTER ONE

1

The invitation to lunch with Sir Charles at his club made my nostrils twitch and brought the thought that he was about to suggest something grotesque. When lunch was light but excellent—oysters, Dover sole, syllabub, asparagus and Stilton—I knew he didn't expect me to go sleepy on him but to keep thinking as keenly as possible. When his whole demeanour became genial I suspected that his suggestion would, very likely, be bad for my health.

We went back to his palatial office in the Government Daimler and there he fired his shot.

'We are very anxious to know about a character who, we think, is in the ranks of your acquaintances,' he said. 'Now we are in great difficulty, because you must have met thousands of people and we don't even know the sex of this person, whom we've codenamed Catkin.'

'Then you must know what Catkin has done,' I said, 'or what he is doing.'

'We have arrived at a guess by general failure to detect another person. When I say "we", I mean the police, Intelligence, Customs and all the odds and sods of the Sniffing-Out game.

'What brought it to a head was a general discussion over the commission of two bullion robberies which have occurred over the last eighteen months. In both cases bullion trucks were hi-jacked, the guard and escorts gassed, chained, gagged, blindfolded and so on. The ambushes appear to have been perfect. In the first case it was a silver-bullion cargo, in the second, gold.

'No trace has ever been found of the vehicles, or the cargoes. There was no sudden appearance of gold or silver on the world market. The trucks might as well have been driven into a black hole and lost forever.'

'Which they weren't,' I said. 'But obviously the police, their special divisions, Interpol and all the rest of the set-up have had their go at solving these two jobs. What, therefore, could you possibly want me to do?'

'Wait. After a great deal of digging, the police began to link up certain big art robberies, pictures, statuettes—a number of effects of great value. They too vanished and have never appeared in any sale anywhere at all.'

'Surely we aren't harking back to the mad American millionaire with a secret basement where he's got all Michelangelo's works by theft, and is even keeping the old man alive and well and still at work?'

2

'No mad millionaires,' he said. 'They don't steal bullion, do they? They've got it all. And they prefer oil in the back garden, I believe. No. But you see, we can't believe all this stuff is being hoarded. We think it's being used as barter for something else.'

'Such as arms? A portable version of a bomb? A threat to the world as we know it?'

'I should have lunched you on something less digestible, Jonathan. You are not worrying enough.'

'So far, Charles, you have given several good reasons for the police to recruit more men. I don't delve in police matters. You know that. We—'

'No we, Jonathan. Not your partner and the rest of your jolly firm. Just you this time. We have found that when back-up is supplied to help an agent, it is the back-up which is the weakest security link. In this case we suspect— but we've nothing firm to suggest this—that if we had a success and got somewhere on the trail of this loot we might find ourselves up against diplomatic immunity.'

'Not KGB again?'

'My dear Jonathan, the KGB is not very secret to us, is it? Catkin is an enigma, something new. Something we haven't come across before. In both hi-jackings the operation was carried out with such precision and speed, such a sweep-up of any possible clues that every detail must have been planned and rehearsed to a fine point. The art thefts were just a little more than expert burglaries. They were perfect. There was no mark left behind except the light patch on the wall where the Reynolds used to hang.'

'And no signature?'

'None. The methods and trade marks of the world's best have been studied, analysed, computerised and all the rest of it and no known thief has worked in this way before.'

'Then it's probably a known expert who's had his idiosyncrasies shaved off,' I said.

'More than likely, but very difficult to get hold of.'

There was a pause as Miss Rickenbaker, the secretary, brought in a most elegant tray of teas. Silver itself and with the load of silver and fine china it carried, it might have been worth the attention of Catkin.

'Why these thoughts on diplomatic freedom?' I said when she had gone. 'You must have a line there.'

'You must have friends in embassies, consulates, wharfside diplomatic agencies? You know the sort of thing.'

'Not friends, that I know of. Acquaintances, yes. But not friends. And I hope I'm not being asked to start chasing a friend of mine, because I draw the line.'

'Oh no, we're not asking that, dear boy.'

'Do you know what *you* are asking?'

'Jonathan, what we have done is this. It's

obvious that to carry out these robberies and then vanish the loot, a hiding place is needed, big enough for articulated lorries, amongst other things, so we have listed big estates which have changed hands in recent years, factory complexes which have gone empty—all that sort of spacious privacy which seems in this case to be necessary.'

'You have this list?'

'You can see the file—to memorise.'

'And then I go on an extended tour of the British Isles, taking weeks, wasting weeks? What are you thinking about, Charles? You must have more than you say.'

He brought a file from the top drawer of his desk and handed it across. I glanced through it, but it looked like a land agent's list of vacant properties.

'This is only any good once there is a clue to what Catkin is up to.' I put it back on the desk. 'I take it that Catkin is credited with all these burglaries and hold-ups because of the lack of clues in every case?'

'The police say that the no-sign is his signature. That's the only thing that joins the lot together.'

'Has anybody been hurt?'

'No. It appears the trucks ran into what looked like a mist patch on the road—you know how they form in pretty regular places— only it wasn't mist but knock-out gas. It caused headaches, that's all.'

5

'Any traces of this gas?'

'Uninteresting. Nothing new. Nothing that hasn't been used before, except an additive which keeps it lying low instead of flying up and drifting into the clouds. That's been used before, too, in military tests.'

'So he's got a chemist, would you say?'

'We think he has several experts covering a range of useful subjects.'

'Diplomatic immunity,' I said.

'Worries you, that, doesn't it? But it's been suggested we might come up against it, because in that case, things would become very difficult for us. So we must consider it.'

'Yes, but how did it arise?'

'The suggestion? I don't know. I imagine it was just at a conference of several officers who were kicking ideas around, and that came up as a frustration ploy. To make everybody mad, I guess.'

'Somebody suggested it, and I always think there is a reason, even if it goes back into a childhood experience.'

'I'd hate to go into the childhood of senior police officers,' Charles said.

I sat and looked at him.

'Consider it all,' I said. 'I would go from here now as wise as I came in. I have nothing whatever to go on, nowhere to start. You must have some clue, just for a starter. Give me that, and I've got a key which helps to find a door.'

'It's somebody you know and who knows you,' he said again. 'Not in the distant past, but in the last few years.'

'But one gets to know new people every day!'

He looked at me quizzically.

'Do you meet new people every day who have an ambition to set themselves up as top criminal organisations and can afford to get the best in the world and also to pay to have their nasty habits erased?'

'How would I tell what a man's secret ambition is? If it turned out to be one like you say, he surely wouldn't tell me. There was a crackpot woman once—a writer, broadcaster, you know the sort, never stops talking—but she was an oddball with no sign of wealth. She used to have some theory that any clever person could hoodwink the rest of the world— not some of the time, but all the time, but after she'd talked for three hours it dawned on me she was trying to get out of me how I would do it. She wanted it for a crime story.'

'Perhaps she sold her idea to somebody who carried it out.'

'It needed more than an idea. Hers was more a wish than anything else.'

'Still, it's a spark,' Charles said. 'Or have you another fancy?'

'An art collector perhaps,' I said. 'And there is a tenuous connection between those— usually—gentlemen and Miss Rachel Gorm.'

'Gorm?' said Charles.

'As in gormless, but she is far from that.'

'She could start someone thinking?'

'Anyone can be a trigger for an idea. The problem is to make the idea into something practical.' I looked at him. 'Charles, from what you say I have the idea that you or the baffled investigators have already, hopefully, sided me with someone I know pretty well, not in the past, but recently, if not now.'

'Lord Legges.'

'Bernard?' I said, and thought a moment. 'Well he made a fortune from gumboots, but he never made any. It was a financial deal, like all his other deals, but as for crime—it doesn't really suit him. Why Legges?'

'That was a suggestion that came out of a kick-about round the conference table.'

'Oh, you talked about me there?'

'You and an awful lot of others. Just names at the time, remember. There was nothing to go on.'

'Bernard has a town house and a country estate,' I said. 'And the latter was burgled for art treasures, in the course of which his wife was murdered, and the general public were not quite sure who did the murder. The thieves weren't caught and the loot never went into the black market and it was assumed that they were scared that if they sold it that would lay a direct line to them for the police to follow.'

'Yes,' said Charles. 'But a number of other

country houses were done round about that time, and there was violence in two of those cases.'

'I didn't know that. But I do know this; Bernard would be the last person in the world to steal bullion and then do nothing about it.'

'You could start there. He knows a great many people.'

'A lot of art collectors, business men, chiefs of multi-nationals. Yes. He knows an awful lot of people. But I am of the opinion, Charles, that he is a born coward. I don't see him risking his all as a master crook.'

'But he might know someone who would.'

'And he might even put money in behind him if he thought it would be profitable,' I said.

We laughed then, but I realised that the opening period of vagueness was over.

'You want me to look at him with a view to getting a lead?' I said.

'You're an outsider, you know him, you know what we are talking about here, and it's a lead we're asking for, not Legges in chains. By the way where does his title come from?'

'From a duck pond,' I said.

'Rubbish!' he laughed.

'Not a bit of rubbish. For some reason his grandfather named a duckpond outside the back door of his little country cottage. He named it Legges, and put up a stone which he carved himself. It's still there, stone and pond together. The cottage has gone but Bernard owns the land. He drags the pond for old bicycles and bedsteads every year. It's a great little area for pond life.'

'Which is just what I would like you to study,' said Charles. 'Pond life, weeds, lizards, toads. Big toads, small toads, frogs, just in case there's one who wants to blow up all the others and take over as ruler of Nobody.'

'You really think it that serious?' I said.

'There are some of us here who are dead scared of it. I'd like you to join in.'

'Join in getting scared?'

'Why should you miss poignant suffering?'

'If it leads on, what about back-up?'

'I told you, we mustn't take risks. We will give you back-up when you find out who Catkin is. From that moment, you step out.'

'I hope I do.'

2

I left Charles with what I felt was a handful of nothing. Not that he could have given any more than he had; he just hadn't got it. The reason why he had asked me, I guessed, was that once, in a case which had puzzled the whole establishment, I had fallen on the solution by accident which had been mistaken for divine inspiration.

I thought he was hoping, as a last resort, that it could happen again.

I am not a patient man. If I am pointed towards a suspect, my natural tendency is to go direct and ask him.

I went to see Bernard, Lord Legges, at his London house. He was a tall, thin, almost sharp featured man with very quick blue eyes that always looked as if they were going somewhere else.

'My dear boy!' he said, when I went into his large study. 'This is a surprise. What now?'

'I want some advice, Bernard,' I said.

'You were always a one to come straight to the point,' he said. 'Never waste time asking after health; it spends a minute that could be making money!' He laughed.

'I can see you're well. You can see I am. I have been fidgeting about, wondering over this Atlantic Heron stock.'

'You want to play your assets?' he said. 'Of course. How much Heron have you got?'

I told him.

'Too much. The time to spread it about is now.' He went on talking about the markets, what to risk and where. Some brokers said he was a genius, others that he was a lucky punter, but one thing I was sure of, he studied his gambles acutely before he placed a bet.

After we had chatted on a few other things he invited me to his country place for a couple of days.

'I'm trying a new ploy,' he said. 'You'd be interested. A medium.'

11

'A medium?' I said, surprised.

'You wouldn't know, but after my wife died I tried for a while to get in touch. Obviously, that's not the sort of thing I push around outside, but you're a man I think would be very interested indeed in this sort of thing.'

He stood up and went to the window, then turned back to me.

'I didn't get in touch, but this woman contacted other—spirits or ghosts, or whatever they are—and one dear departed, who had been a financier started giving tips. For the fun of it, I tried the advice he gave, and it came off. It came off several times.'

'Is the medium the sort of woman to be interested in the Stock Markets?'

'Maria Bragg? I ask you! No, she has more the character of a fairground fortune-teller, but she just happens to have something they haven't.'

Well, Charles had said get in with him because he was suspect, so I got in and accepted the invitation. I arrived at Legges Court, Hertfordshire, on the Wednesday afternoon. There were two other guests, a German woman, Magda Hirsch, and an overseas sales representative for an engineering firm, James Ball.

James Ball was in a moody state and wandered about clutching a cut-glass Jacobean tumbler full of Scotch against his waistcoat. He looked as if he had failed to sell anything for several months, if not years.

He was terse, uncommunicative. I didn't bother to get anything out of him, but it did occur to me that his gruff attitude might have been due to the fact he had heard of me before. I was a partner in a firm of industrial investigators, and perhaps he didn't like that sort of thing.

Magda Hirsch was dark and very full of figure. Her eyes were green and very penetrating. She talked without much restraint. She had come from Dresden, and her family had been rich manufacturers, but now they were all poor under the Socialist regime and were treated like pig manure, which is why she had left, she said.

'You know about this séance?' she said.

'Yes. Bernard told me.'

'It is only lately he has told anybody,' she said. 'He was keeping secrets, but now he is using it for business. Clever, ha?'

'Original, perhaps. Have you joined in a séance before?'

'Yes. Once I was at one. It was a fraud.'

'Did you find that out for sure?' Ball suddenly interrupted, as if he had surfaced from a bad dream.

'It was exposed. It was all exposed. It was pitiful. It had been very creepy till then, but up jumps this man and shines a torch and there is another woman behind the curtain with a white face and all that. It was very stupid.'

13

Ball looked at me, then went away to where there was a tray with drinks on it. He took up a Scotch bottle.

'This will not be stupid,' Magda went on, 'because it is here, you see, in the man's house where she cannot fix it with lots of curtains and all that. You can hide such a lot of people behind curtains, isn't that so?'

I agreed.

'Is she here now, Maria Bragg?'

'No. I think the chauffeur is sent for her just before the sitting. She does not like to get mixed up with the people before, though Bernard says she is all right after and with a few drinks to steady her up.'

'Does she go into trances?' I said.

'After the trinks? Ja!' Magda laughed, then became serious. 'No, I don't know what she does at these things. I say I have been only to a dud one. A fraud, you know.'

Magda was very charming, but I still had time to wonder what I was really doing here. Everything was above board, as far as I could see, there was no room to hide articulated trucks or even the one-piece variety, unless they were stacked in woods at the rear of the estate. But I don't believe such things can be hidden for more than a few days in places where people like gamekeepers, poachers, or just small boys can normally go. There were garages and stables around the building, but no barns or other large places of temporary

14

concealment, at least for big lorries.

Bernard had been in his library, making and taking phone calls to brokers, markets, industrial tipsters and anybody else who could advance his fortune even by a penny.

He joined us just before dinner, which was a meal typical of the great loves from his past; boiled beef and carrots, dumplings, pease pudding, onions, boiled potatoes, followed by jam tart and custard, Cheddar and water biscuits. A meal for the 'conoozer of the house-by-the-duckpond', as he styled himself once. The 'table wine' was beer, port with the cheese.

The net result of this old English feast was that after it our critical faculties were not so sharp when it came to joining in the fantasies of Maria Bragg.

The séance took place in a room which was small by comparison with the others on the ground floor. It had two tall windows with long brown velvet curtains reaching to the polished floor outside the silk carpet. There was a circular table in the middle of the room with a baize top of billiard-table green. There were four chairs arranged around with a carved oak armchair at the head, which of course, it formed by being larger than the other chairs.

In the centre was a silk-shaded table lamp.

We sat round as directed by Bernard, myself on the medium's left next to Magda, who was next to Ball—who had said nothing at all about séances—next to Bernard, on the medium's right.

The room lights were switched off, leaving only the shaded table lamp, so shaded that it left our faces in a kind of pale gloom while it lit the baize of the table with a brilliant glow.

We all sat there, waiting, and perhaps wondering, and often glancing at the empty chair.

'It has to be the right moment for her to make her entrance,' Bernard explained, in quiet, almost whispering, tones. 'It's a matter of temperament.'

Ball grunted. Magda looked at me across the upper dusk.

'It's for effect, not temperament,' said Ball, gruffly, but quietly.

'It's an atmosphere of impending doom,' I said, to lighten the odd sort of tension that I could feel growing between us.

'Maybe yours, dear boy,' said Bernard.

Magda made a curious little noise like a gulp.

'Your supper's give me the bloody burps,' she said.

The door opened, and Maria Bragg came in. Her head was above the reach of the shaded lamp, but I could see she wore a long dark cloak and some sort of white dress underneath. She did not speak or look at anyone, but sat down in the armchair, and for a minute or so sat there, head bent as if in

16

prayer.

Then she raised her head and made a signal with her hand towards Bernard.

In that moment I saw her face in the gloom, and I was sure I had met her before, but not in the name of Maria Bragg.

CHAPTER TWO

1

We laid our hands on the table, little fingers touching. We sat like that for almost a minute, then Maria Bragg took her hands off the table, lifted my right hand and Bernard's left and put them on the table again with little fingers touching. She then sat back, her face entirely in shadow and laid her hands on top of Bernard's and mine as they touched.

'Yes,' the medium said.

Bernard operated a foot switch and the light went out. We sat in darkness for what seemed a long time. The atmosphere became tense. I seemed to feel the high frequencies of almost fearful expectation filling the black air round the four sitters. It is said that animals can smell fear, but I think it is more likely that they sense the frequency transmissions of fear, as I could sense it then.

At first Maria's hand was steady as it lay on mine, but slowly I began to detect a faint trembling, and I felt a physical tension in my right hand from it.

The sensations running between our hands did not seem like any recognisable part of practised trickery; something was causing a reaction in Maria Bragg.

Again I tried to remember where and when I had seen her before and who she had been nominally. The faint trembling seemed to become more intense.

Suddenly the hand was taken from mine.

'No!' the medium said. 'There's an opposition.'

The lamp came on again, brilliantly lighting the outspread hands on the table.

'Break the circle,' she said. 'This is useless.'

'Is it someone?' Bernard asked.

'It's in the air. I don't know where,' Maria said and put her fingers to her forehead.

'It might be better later?' Bernard said.

'Perhaps.' She closed her eyes. 'It is disturbing me.'

'One of us, perhaps?' Magda said, eyes big with curiosity so the whites were clear in the shadow.

Maria shook her head, her eyes still closed, then touched her fingers to her temples.

'No, it is not present in the solid. It is something else.'

'Have you sat in here before?' I said.

'No. It's new. There is something—I can't place it. Dead—undead—I can't tell.'

'Someone going to die?' Magda suggested.

The woman did not open her eyes but her head kept still, yet without moving or speaking she seemed to reject the suggestion. It was such a strange way of communicating what we all understood without seeing or hearing any

19

movement or word from her.

I began to doubt that she was some spoof expert whom I had come across before. I might have been mistaking a superficial likeness. That would explain why I couldn't place her.

Or was she making me doubt myself? Or was I suffering, like so many do, from fear of the unknown?

Or perhaps, I thought in a lighter strain, the weight of boiled beef and carrots was a little too much for my digestion to cope with when troubled by a séance.

'Do you want to try again?' Bernard said. He didn't ask in the tone of one sympathising with her disturbed self, but as one impatient to get on with it for his benefit, if for nobody else's.

'Is it necessary for everybody to be dead in the mood?' Ball grumbled. 'If so, why not press on until the mood arrives. Treat it like sex. Organise it. Don't pant around; make it come to you.'

'There is a crude man,' said Magda, watching him. 'You cannot make things come to you without a lot of money.'

'Count me out,' Ball said. 'I'm stony. But what I mean is, what's the good of lighting up and getting rattled because it didn't happen first time? Try again. Stick on trying. That way something'll come. It has to.'

'What do you think, Maria?' said Bernard.

'Go again?'

The woman was still sitting, eyes closed, fingers on her temples, as if she heard nothing at all of what we were saying.

Bernard stared at her and put out a hand as if to wake her up. I reached across and stopped him before he touched her.

'Wait!' I said.

Reluctantly he drew his hand back. He stared hard at her, so did Magda. Ball seemed to become aware of the brief tension we could feel building up very slowly. I don't think Ball believed anything that was out of the ordinary. Anything unusual, for him, had to exist a long time before he recognised it and by then it was ordinary.

'She is in trance,' Magda whispered to me. 'Should we put our hands together?'

'Don't do anything,' I said. 'Just wait.'

I believed that she had drifted into some kind of waking sleep, and I have always heard it to be dangerous if such sleepers are shocked into wakefulness. It may have been fool's talk but I felt it best not to test it.

Whatever state she was in, Maria Bragg was not then with us. That much was obvious.

We waited. Now and again, somebody whispered, then quiet fell once more.

The voice began almost as if whispering at a distance, but then became stronger. Maria's eyes were still shut and her hands had fallen into her lap. Her head was half-turned, lying against the high back of the chair. Her lips moved.

'He wants to know. That is why he comes. He wants to *know*.'

It was not her voice. It was a man's voice. The voice of a man which troubled my memory more than her looks had done. She repeated the words, as if the spirit was trying to reach someone else at the table.

'Will you say more?' Bernard whispered, as if he spoke to someone standing behind the chair. 'Will you say more!'

'He knows, but will know more.'

The voice was clear then and I remembered where I had heard it before. The man had been lying on the floor, half twisted, his head slightly raised, looking at me.

'You turned too soon,' he had said, gasping. 'You always turn—too bloody—soon!'

And then he had died. I had shot him with a wound that had killed him in a very few minutes. I had heard him come behind me and my turning had shaken his aim. He missed. I didn't.

And he was dead. He had been dead for years.

Maria sat in the chair, speaking with his voice again. He had come back to speak, to play one more dirty trick, perhaps, for revenge.

'What does he say?' Bernard whispered urgently. 'What does he mean?'

I looked aside. Magda's eyes were big, but

she seemed to be looking at me. It was Ball who looked really bad.

He stared at the heavy lampshade as if his eyes would fall from their sockets. His hands grabbed the table so his knuckles stood out hard and white.

Then suddenly he jumped up.

'Bloody fraud!' he cried. 'Bloody, bloody fraud!'

He turned away from the table and went to the door.

Bernard turned his head and looked towards him.

'Come back!' he shouted.

Maria groaned. Bernard jumped up as if to stop Ball leaving. Magda took hold of my hand suddenly and held it very tight as if fearing something bad would happen.

I saw Maria come suddenly wide awake.

'This is a trick!' she cried and sat forward. 'I can't go on with this.'

Maria gathered her cloak round her and got up. Both Ball and Bernard turned to look at her as she walked with long strides up to and past them. She opened the door and went out of the room, leaving the door wide behind her.

2

'What the hell's going on?' Bernard said, blankly.

'You know what's going on!' shouted Ball.

'It's bloody tricks going on. This is a fake. All of it! A fake! That voice was a trick. He's dead! Randers is dead!'

'Stop shouting!' Bernard said. His tone was nasty, to say the least. His reputation was one of sharpness to the point of the vicious, and he certainly showed some of this quality then.

Ball stood back, staring at Bernard with wide eyes.

'You know what I mean,' he said. 'You knew Randers.'

'Randers has been dead five years,' Bernard said, coldly. 'Don't talk such rubbish. What did you think she would do then? Deal with the spirits who're alive? Don't be a fool, man! Don't you realise what she was trying to do? She did it, that's all!'

Magda held my hand still, and she bent her head closer to me.

'It was real?' she whispered, big-eyed.

'Bernard has just said it was,' I said, carefully. 'Somebody called Randers.'

'I din' think it would be going to work,' she said, and shrugged as she took her hand away at last. 'I don't like it much.'

'What did you expect?'

'Not somebody who would scare people out of their conscience,' she said quietly. 'It would seem like a rig-up.'

She looked towards the two men by the door.

'Have a drink,' Bernard said, his anger

24

apparently evaporating. 'We'll all have a drink. We have become overawed with the business because, all of a sudden, some of us knew who was talking, and it wasn't somebody we wanted. That's the trouble. Nobody wants the ghost of Banquo at the feast.'

He was pouring drinks from a table in the corner as he spoke because, to cover the uneasiness in that room, he wanted to be moving, to shift the atmosphere out of tension.

Magda watched the two men as if she found them more interesting than the psychic phenomena that had come to pass at the table. Both men were clearly shaken. As far as I was concerned, the name Randers was new to me, but the well-remembered gentleman who had tried to murder me had used many names to my knowledge. Randers would do as well as any of the others.

Maria Bragg had sat quite motionless, apparently unconscious in the chair. Only her lips had moved when the voice of the dead man had come out of them.

One of Randers' activities had been blackmail, and one of his methods the sending of anonymous tapes, so that quite a few recordings of his voice must have been left behind after his sudden end. Anyone could have got hold of one or more if they had wanted to copy his voice.

Maria Bragg could have carried out her imitation by using such tapes and learning them carefully. The changing of the voice from her own to Randers' was the difficult part, but with a natural mimic there would be no problem.

She could be a natural mimic, an actress—

That thought brought me back to my original question of where I might have seen her before. I remembered a woman called Sonia who had impersonated men on stage in Brussels. Hers had been a comic act, rude in parts, and ended with her stripping down to her shoes thus revealing the final surprise that she wasn't a man at all.

I had been investigating a case of industrial espionage and had traced a leak to Brussels. In that case a man's voice had been used on telephone calls to Sheffield in imitation of the real Belgian representative.

We had got nowhere with Sonia. She had known nothing about anything and only dimly understood what a telephone was, as she had been brought up in a convent run by nuns with beards. Her act with us had been of such dumb innocence that we gave up the line of inquiry, before we went potty.

In the end we found we had no need to get help from her because we found the guilty party soon after.

It was the gift of imitating the male voice, which was so unlike her own, which brought her to mind, and also the likeness between her and Maria Bragg. There was definitely a physical resemblance, but I couldn't have sworn the two women were one and the same.

'Did you understand what she talked about?' Magda spoke quietly but directly at the two men.

Bernard turned quickly, Ball only slowly, as if he didn't want to look at Magda at all.

'It was too general,' Bernard said. 'It could have applied to anything, or anyone.'

'A lot of crap,' Ball said. 'Anyone could have done that. Gabber, that's all. Sort of message that can fit anything.'

I had not felt like that about it. I had thought it applied directly to me and my visit to that place.

I was surprised to find that Ball might have the same reaction and I began to wonder just what he had come for. He had said something about being 'off for Saudi' the following night. Perhaps he was, and if so, then he had come to this place for something and expected to get it in under twenty-four hours.

From what I knew of Bernard he wouldn't be persuaded into any new business in twenty-four hours, so maybe Ball's interest in this place was something different from a business scheme.

'You men are funny,' Magda said, looking to the three of us, one after the other. 'You have this medium, she contacts with the Other World and you don't give a damn. "Have a drink, old man", you say as if a drink is more important than what she did for you.'

'Magda, my dear,' said Bernard, smiling graciously, 'you mustn't take these things too seriously. That way madness lies. Look on it as an entertainment. I like it because it gives me ideas. From ideas I make money. That is my work.'

'You are a Philistine,' Magda said. 'But why do you have her if you take no notice?'

'She wasn't on form,' Bernard said coolly. 'You see, my dear Magda, I employ her to get certain results and there were none forthcoming tonight.'

'How do you know for sure?'

'Because I know her. Now let's have done with it.'

'Pig,' said Magda calmly and turned to me. 'Do you play chess, Mr Blake?'

'I do, but I'm no good at it.'

'You forgive,' she said, got up and walked out of the room.

'An impulsive girl,' I said, going to the table. 'What does she do?'

'A bloody investigative journalist,' Bernard said, with a nasty edge to his voice. 'Think they've a right to bust in on anybody's privacy and nose round his underwear cupboard looking for revelations. Look how the Americans copped it. Lost a President and found themselves stranded with the morals of *The Washington Post*.'

'Keen on morals, are you?' said Ball,

peering at him.

'Hate 'em,' said Bernard, briefly.

Bernard was upset, I thought perhaps his séance had misfired, but séances are only dependable when they are rigged, and if one was rigged it wouldn't be any good to Bernard.

He said he got business tips from spiritual utterings. I didn't believe that, but I did believe he had something from them and Maria's failure that night had been a big disappointment.

What had he expected that he wanted us to hear?

He didn't like any of us or our occupations, so the séance must have been arranged as some kind of show-off, but it had flopped and he was angry about it.

Ball had also shown signs of anger and I assumed it was for the same reason; that he had expected something that hadn't happened.

Magda, whose job it was to pick up any and every scrap of what did happen, had been unaffected by failure—if such it had been, although I thought that what Maria had done had been very good and effective.

It had made me feel most uneasy, but for the fact that I felt sure the performance was rigged. If it had been, then Maria had rigged it on her own, otherwise Bernard would not have been angry with her performance.

'I thought Maria Bragg was ill,' I said. 'Is she alone?'

Bernard looked at me almost with anger.

'She has a maid with her,' he said shortly.

I went to the door.

'The nearest is the main hall?' I queried.

'Yes. Just along to the right.' Bernard stared morosely into his brandy.

I went out into the corridor and closed the door behind me. It was quiet, but the whispering sound of a woman's voice came from somewhere. I walked slowly along on the thick carpet, listening.

Another woman's voice spoke, fainter than the first. I traced it to a door across the corridor, and knocked lightly on the panels. A girl called 'Come in!'

I went in. The small room had been got together as a temporary dressing room, with a table, long mirror, an armchair, a sofa and two smaller chairs.

Maria Bragg was lying back on the sofa, head turned to look at the caller. Behind the sofa, and obviously interrupted in the act of watching herself in the mirror, was a fat blonde girl. Her head was screwed round so she could see me over her right shoulder, then she turned fully towards me and smiled.

Maria glared at me.

'Sorry to butt in,' I said, 'but I think we've met before, Miss Bragg.'

'If we have, I've forgotten,' she said. 'What do you want?'

'We met in Brussels,' I said. 'About five

years ago.'

'Funny,' she said, shaking her head slowly. 'I've never been to Brussels. Now go away.'

She did not look at me as she spoke, but held her forehead as if suffering a headache.

'You didn't finish your message,' I said.

I looked at the fat girl, she smiled back, and looked as if she would be ready to tell me anything, given privacy.

'My message?' Maria looked up sharply. 'What message is this?'

'Why, the one you started to give when you were entranced. Or isn't that the right way to put it?'

'Alice, give me three minutes,' Maria said and waved a hand.

Alice did not mind but came round the corner, her smile warming as she came towards me. I opened the door for her and she winked at me as she passed by and out into the corridor.

Maria looked at me with a hard stare.

'What do you want?' she said.

'To renew an old acquaintance.'

'Just who are you?'

'With your powers, you should know. Didn't Bernard tell you?'

She stared along to her feet at the end of the sofa.

'He just said names. They mean nothing. Why do you keep saying Brussels?'

'You did a cabaret there, when you were

called Sonia.'

Suddenly she laughed, but there was no humour in it.

'I have a sister,' she said. 'She had a show in Brussels. She became mistress to the Duc de Something. Gave up stage for age, you could say. But he's rich. That's why.'

'I'm sorry. I was mistaken. I would like to say I was impressed tonight.'

'Thank you.'

'Does Bernard often ask your help?'

'Look, are you some ruddy journalist or something?'

'No. Bernard is trying to interest me in one of his new deals. I'm looking for a check. I never like losing a lot of money through being careless.'

Her interest flickered a little brighter as I mentioned 'a lot of money'.

'He says you advise him,' I said.

'He may say so,' she answered. 'I wouldn't know.'

'Yes, I understand that. But you contact people who were in finance, and he must mention names which you have given, without knowing you have.'

'He does mention them—sometimes—but they were all business contacts of his when they were alive. He often says who I'm supposed to try for. That craps it up, usually. I can't work like a phone dial.'

'When did you find you could do this?'

'My mother was psychic. Things like that run in families.'

'It must be mentally exhausting.'

'It empties me right out, usually.'

'But not now, you mean?'

'I didn't get through tonight,' she said. 'It was a fail.'

'You did say some things, but not business things.'

'Sometimes you can get on the edge of something when concentrating, but it doesn't usually mean anything.'

Meaning, I thought, that she is changing her mind about me and it was probably the remark 'a lot of money' which had fired her imagination.

'Didn't you know you said something tonight—in a strange male voice?'

'No. I can't tell. It's not my brain working. It's used as an agent. I give it.'

'But you must have had tapes and heard them?'

'The voices don't record on tapes.'

'What?'

'Bernard tried when I asked him to. Nothing came out. He looked pretty ghastly when he ran it through. He kept on, because he couldn't believe it. Then he accused me of tricks! Scatty bastard! How on earth could I fake his tapes when I'm in a trance?'

'You couldn't,' I said, agreeably. 'But Bernard likes everything his way.'

She looked keenly at me.

'What did I say tonight?' she said.

'Well, you said something which shook me, because it was just like the voice of a man who stole a quarter of a million from me. A man called Dusty Randers, amongst other names.'

Her eyes grew big, then froze into icy diamonds.

'The evil skunk!' she shouted. 'The double-crossing thug!'

Then she lay back as if exhausted by frustration, because what can you do to punish a dead man?

CHAPTER THREE

1

Maria Bragg was very angry over the story I had told her about Dusty Randers. She said quite a lot to his discredit until one last phrase suddenly made her realise how incongruous was her vilification.

'I'll murder the—' There she stopped.

Apparently the fact that Randers had been dead some years had temporarily slipped her memory, or else her continued hobnobbing with the spirits of the departed removed from her mind the usual deference to *nil nisi bonum.*

'He never told me anything about money like that,' she said, still angry but more rational. 'Still, it's gone now, I suppose.' She frowned. 'What I could never understand was how he could have killed himself with a gun accident. He was used to guns. He'd been in the army till he got thrown out. Yet there he went and slipped or something happened and he shot himself.'

'Accidents do happen,' I said. 'People get over-confident.'

I remembered him then as I had turned, sensing someone behind me, and he had been there, the pistol pointing at me and a smile on his face. He had been prepared to carry out the execution slowly, but my sudden turning made him pause just enough to let me fire first, so that when he pulled his trigger he was already hit and his aim was off centre. But he smiled on, even as he died standing, and when he had collapsed and fallen, the smile had still been on his mouth. As if he hadn't really minded being dead.

And remembering him then I wondered if he had really cared about anything. Risking death had been a part of his life; salt and pepper on his daily bread.

'He was a friend of yours?' I said.

'You could say that. He had great charm and sophistication. His trouble was he couldn't keep away from the idea of getting money, easily, and very quickly. He was not a violent man, but where money was concerned, violence might have been an incidental way of getting it. Or—' she shook her head in doubt, '—perhaps violence just increased the risk he was taking and he never could resist increasing the risks.'

'I wonder how it came about you used his voice tonight?' I said.

'He could have been in my mind at that moment,' she said, slowly. 'One never entirely forgets people one's known very well.'

'Did you ever work together?'

She sat straight.

'You're getting very inquisitive!'

'Not really. But you were so angry that

Randers never told you about the money he had from me. Naturally that's a matter of interest to me.'

She sat still, staring. She was angry, but for some reason it softened and she relaxed again.

'It was an idea he had about doing visits to country houses, holding séances to private order—'

'As you do now.'

'Well—yes. But his idea was that I should spy out the land and leave things unlocked for him to walk in later and gather up the proceeds. Robbing the place, in short.'

'You wouldn't go along with that.'

'Not likely! What's the good of working up a wealthy connection and then robbing it? It's the golden egg and goose syndrome. I want a steady income, not one wild bust and then inside for a five-year rest.'

She got off the sofa and started looking round.

'It's time I went home,' she said. 'I don't hang about after good shows, and certainly not after flops.'

'Do you live near here?'

'No. I've got a motor caravan, but I don't show it to customers. Smacks a bit of gypsy, don't you think? I just get a lift away from the performance area, drop off at some convenient point and walk the rest. It makes 'em think. Adds to the mystic aura.'

'Thanks for talking.'

She gave me a road map of the area.

'The house,' she said, pointing to the map, 'is here. The motorvan—' she traced a line along a road, then a lane and stopped at a wood almost at the back of Bernard's estate, '—is there.'

She looked at me, I looked at her, then we smiled, and she turned and went about getting her things together. As I left the room the fat girl went back into it as if by a system of thought-catching she had known when to arrive.

Or it could have been a simpler system, such as keyhole listening.

2

'Been chatting up the busty seer?' said Bernard, with a faintly unpleasant sneer, or perhaps it was meant to be a leer.

'You know such things fascinate me. That's why you asked me.'

'No,' he said shortly. 'I asked you so you could spot the fake, but she was too clever. She called it off.'

'She was upset. But she has worked for you before, you said.'

'Yes, yes. Given some good tips. Sometimes she's really scared me, and what scares me most is that she doesn't seem to remember anything after.'

'And the voices don't record on the tapes?'

He looked at me shaprly.

'That's right,' he said. 'They don't.'

'Where are the others?'

'Magda is trying to seduce Ball, but he's trying to seduce himself with a Scotch bottle. She won't win.'

'He has to fly off tomorrow.'

'So he says. But he needn't. I've made him an offer which he is supposed to be considering through a haze of burnside spirit. I shall withdraw the offer. A drunk isn't reliable.'

'Why did you make it?'

'He is a very experienced man. A traveller of distinction in half the world. It's just that his ulcers seem to be getting the better of him.'

'Bernard, you invited him because you wanted to use him, and you'll bloody well use him, because that's the sort of hard villain you are,' I said, and added, 'My glass is empty.'

'Jonathan, when it comes to villainy, I never know where to award the marks. Help yourself. Or—if you insist—I will.'

'I insist,' I said. 'I never give myself enough, out of politeness.'

He helped me. I watched his hands holding the glass under the syphon of soda. There was a slight tremor. He was either angry or worried.

'Why are you against me, Jonathan?' he said, without looking round.

'I am always an independent, Bernard,' I

39

said. 'And I don't like the idea of you getting me here in order to prove the girl is a fake.'

'I don't like that idea, either,' he said drily. 'She isn't a fake. But somebody here is. Which one is what I wanted you to find out.'

'Out of two people?'

'So it would seem.'

'But from my angle, there are three. After all, Bernard, we are all fakes at one time or another. It depends on what suits the opportunity presented, surely?'

'Sometimes you have an extraordinary vision of morality, Jonathan.'

'It's a variable vision. In this case I can't see what you're after. Why a medium to foresee—not with any great certainty—what you can get from your normal contacts in the markets? It doesn't make sense to me.'

'You're digging.'

'How else do you get the potatoes?'

'I have no spuds to give, but you can guess if you like.'

'I think you're bored with your companies and investments. I think you're going for something entirely new and the idea of calling in Maria Bragg is to try and see what the signs, portents, influences and stars are doing in your favour or against it.'

'You were always a man of imagination.'

'There's no imagination about this. You know perfectly well that if you've got something new to unload on the business

40

world there are words and winds blowing about some time before the advent of the launching. This time there's nothing.'

He looked at me steadily.

'Isn't there some old saying about Other times, Other methods? French or something.'

'Or something,' I said.

We were then in a big room furnished more like a club smoking-room than any room in a private house. There was a big television. Bernard went and switched it on. Stock market prices began to write out across the screen, giving the latest movements on Wall Street.

He watched the screen for a short time.

'What's Gold?' I said, and sat down to look at the fireplace.

'Up five dollars. It'll go higher. That little war in Afrobangoria or whatever it is. Every time there's a new little war people get nervous about paper money. Another drink?'

'No thanks. I'm rather tired. It's all this psychic strain. The air's buzzing with ghosts.'

'Sarcastic rotter,' said Bernard and laughed. 'I'll watch some more of the tape.'

He flicked the tape back to the start of the day's movements on Wall Street and applied himself to a study of what had happened.

I went up to my room. Bernard was watching market movements, a customary occupation for him, but if some very large disruption of the international status quo could be stage managed he would know precisely where to scoop the money pool within the first five minutes of the disturbance beginning.

Where were the bullion trucks? Somewhere in an innocent house and lands might be a hiding place, but in a country area I thought it would have to be underground. But digging out underground places takes a lot of machinery and there is a mountain of soil to get rid of. That kind of work could not be done without the whole neighbourhood, even the county, knowing all about it.

And there would be scars left on the land. Helicopters are employed to find scars when looking for hiding places. And certainly they looked after each bullion robbery.

The lost trucks could have been broken up into small pieces and lumped away in a scrapyard somewhere. But the main question remained, which was: Why had the bullion and other art treasures not appeared after such a long time?

One obvious fact was that the thieves were rich and didn't need any immediate gain from their crimes. They could afford to wait and hold a fortune until it could be doubled.

Or until it could be spent in some way . . .

There was a soft knocking at the door. I called out for the visitor to come in. Magda appeared, still in her evening gown which had seemed to her suitable for a séance, but looked as if one failure of a stitch would cause an immediate fall-out.

'I want to speak with you,' she said, quietly, and looked round the walls. 'Do you think there is any—listening?' She whispered the word.

'No,' I said.

In fact I knew there wasn't. I carried a small bug-detector and had already tested the room. It may seem a reprehensible thing for a guest to do, but my visit was anything but friendly.

And I was sure, after that evening, that Bernard knew it.

'The séance,' she said, and sat on the dressing-table stool.

'What did you think of it?'

'She did not speak the man's voice,' Magda said.

'Her lips moved. I saw that.'

'Perhaps she was trying to speak, but she did not. The voice came from behind the chair, behind her head.'

'Are you sure of that?'

'Did you ask her about it?'

'No.'

'You spoke with her for some time.'

'I thought I had met her, but it seems she has a sister.'

'So you did not mention what she said in the chair?'

'According to you—what she didn't say in the chair.'

'Very well.'

'She genuinely didn't seem to know she had said anything. It's always possible she may be genuine.'

'Of course. I do not know, one way or the other, but I think she was put out so the voice could be played.'

'You think she was drugged?'

'A little one that works only for a minute or two. There are all sorts now.'

'Yes, I know. But she came into the room alone and sat down. Nobody touched her.'

'I hear she always has a small drink before she starts. A ginger ale. Tastes hot. One would not notice a little something slipped into it, perhaps?'

'You are accusing Bernard of rigging the whole thing so that he could play his tape?'

'Yes.' She looked at me steadily. 'We all knew that voice, did we not?'

I watched her carefully.

'Did you recognise it?'

'Most certainly. It is a man who called himself Randers. I came across him first in Köln, then Stuttgart, then Hamburg. He was all over Germany then. Wherever I went, there he seemed to pop up. He said he was chasing me. It was a good ploy, but it seemed to me more that I was constantly finding him, rather than him chasing me.'

'What was he doing there?'

'He was a traveller, he said. But he was in some kind of racket. I am sure of that, but I could never find out what it was. One night he came to my hotel in Hamburg, and asked me to hide him. He said a vice gang was after him and he needed to stay until three a.m., when the boat left.'

'The boat for where?'

'A freighter for Rio, he said. I felt then he was too frightened to lie. But he went, and I didn't see him again. But in the course of my work I found it wasn't only a vice gang that had been after him, but security men as well. He was spying.'

'Yes. That was one of his sidelines. He was anybody's agent so long as it paid. He adapted that activity so that it provided him with a profitable interest in blackmail. He was a man of many parts.'

She looked at me curiously, her eyes narrowed.

'You knew him well, then?'

'Apparently as well as you did. What about Ball?'

'Yes. They had met—as travellers. Ball didn't say anything to me about him.'

There was a pause. Perhaps we both wondered what the other was thinking.

'So Bernard got us all together and threw the common link into the tape. Only Maria Bragg didn't seem to hear it. But it was deliberately done to bring us all together with a common curiosity. What on earth for? Randers has been dead almost five years.'

'Are you sure?' she said.

'Yes. I remember seeing a report. There was an accident with a gun and he shot himself. There was no doubt who it was. You should ask Miss Bragg. It seems she was his girl friend at the time.'

'Amongst others,' said Magda drily, and looked away to the door. 'It is very interesting, but why has Bernard dragged it all up and tossed it to us like meat to tigers?'

'Tigers! Is that the impression you get?'

'It was meant to stir us up. But why does he do that?'

I was wondering very hard then, because, however devious the wealthy Bernard might be, why the tossing of a long-dead man into the apparent serenity of mind of three people he had brought together in the house that night?

How had he known that we had all been well acquainted with Randers? The answer there, almost certainly, was that Randers had told him.

But it had all been so long ago.

Or had the plot that Charles seemed to fear been working up over all that time?

If it had been going that long then it was surely something very big indeed and something Bernard had found well worth investing in. And with a sharp, rather mean punter like Bernard any scheme would need to have very sound features to attract him at all.

'Ah well,' Magda said, standing up. 'Let us forget the mysteries. As it is a party, it is a party. Let us sample the fleshpots.'

And she dropped her dress off as I had imagined it might fall, rippling to the floor, spilling, almost in one silken shimmer.

3

The morning was fine. I walked alone on the estate, having borrowed a walking stick. I walked for an hour and a half across the parkland into the extensive woods to the north-east of the house and found no trace of any ground having been disturbed for years; many years. Any disruption or eruption caused five years ago or before would still have shown some signs, but there was none.

I came to the northernmost limit of the woods where a thorn hedge formed the boundary. It had been well maintained by a practised hedger, and there were no breaks. Some distance along there was a wooden gate, padlocked. Beyond the gate across a stretch of grass before some beech trees, there was a motor caravan.

I had imagined something of a converted small truck, but this was a six-wheeled monster which had the appearance of being an American import. It looked as if it contained everything except an elevator.

I got over the gate and went towards the

caravan. One door was open. As I approached, the fat girl, Alice, came out and down the steps in a bikini, a vision of Scanty straining against the Odds. With every wobble the sparse material shone from the strain.

'Hallo!' she said, advancing. 'Fancy seeing you! Have you walked all the way from the house? You must be puffed. Come and have a drink and cool off. It's lovely inside. Would you like a shah? We've got a shah. Practically everything in here, you know. Randy Saloon, I call it. Come on up.'

She went on up. I waited a few seconds and looked around the rough land the van was parked on. It seemed like part of a common. In the distance I saw a few red cows shoving a way through the gorse, hunting the little patch of greener grass.

I went up the steps into the caravan. It has always surprised me how small a ship looks from the outside, and how large once you get into it. This caravan was like that. A practical drawing-room on wheels, with other rooms beyond a partition, which seemed a long way down from the entrance we had used.

'You've been walking. Thirsty. Warm day. Beah?'

'Fine,' I said.

She got a bottle from a mahogany cupboard.

'Maria's gone to the village,' Alice said, cheerfully. 'Or was it the town? I get mixed up with these little towns and villages round here. Can't make out what's what. They say some of them swelled during the War, whenever that was, for the shadow factories, whatever they where. Some old chap told me.'

She gave me a beer.

'This is a very comfortable vehicle,' I said.

'It's a flat, almost.'

'How long have you parked here?'

'About a week this time. We've been doing some riding. It doesn't seem to do anything for my fat. Still, it's what you're built like, isn't it? Not a lot you can do. Take the fat off and you sag, and that's worse.'

'You worry too much,' I said.

'Oh, you are nice,' she said, and sat down opposite me. 'You know Maria pretty well, don't you?'

'I thought I did, but I was mistaken. I knew her sister.'

'They look alike, do they? Only I never heard of a sister.'

She gave me a rather odd look when she said that, and then looked aside at the open doorway. As she did that she frowned.

'That's funny!' she said, jumping up. 'What's he doing here?'

She went to the door and looked out, blocking the view. I twisted my neck to try to see out of the window, but couldn't without getting up.

I said, 'Who?' as if it didn't matter much.

'Bernard. And he's climbing the gate. Well, I do declare, as the Afro Queen said to the asp. I didn't think he'd ever climb anything. He's too dead cold—He's coming over here. This gets funnier.'

I sat where I was. I had the curious feeling that, if Bernard had never come to this place while Maria had been parked there, he had come now because he thought I'd gone there.

But why was beyond me. I didn't think he could be jealous of Maria, because he never seemed to have enough passion for jealousy; only for making money.

Then his voice sounded outside. He had apparently stopped.

'Get this bloody van off here!' he snapped. 'Get it moved or I'll have it dragged away!'

'Hang on, hang on!' the girl said. 'Maria isn't here.'

'As soon as she gets back, move it, or I will!'

I stood up then and looked out of the window. Bernard was walking away.

CHAPTER FOUR

1

I watched Bernard climb the gate and go away into the woods. The girl turned to me.

'What's up with him?' she said, blankly. 'Maria won't like that!'

'You say you've been here a week?' I said.

'Bit over, actually. Say ten days. I get vague when every day's the same, as it is in the rural life. Yes, I think it is ten days.'

'And he's never been here before?'

'I don't think he was supposed to know where Maria lived.'

'He doesn't know now, does he? He only saw you.'

'He certainly didn't see you or he wouldn't have bawled off like that. Arrogant old sod.' She went and poured herself a beer. 'I hate sucking cans,' she said. 'Uncivilised lot, people.'

'You say you go riding from here?'

'Yes.'

'Where do you get the horses?'

'Oh, there's a stables, riding school, horse hire, about a mile off. A couple of women run it. It's always women with horses, have you noticed? Must be an affinity somewhere. I have an affinity with a horse. When I'm sitting on one the follower can't tell which back end is mine and which the horse's. My mother's fat, too.'

'Buxom,' I corrected.

'You must be the kindest man,' she said, and raised her glass to me. 'Cheers and thanks.'

'Where have you been riding?'

'Oh, all over the place. There's a terrible lot of open ground round here. Quite lovely, really.' She went to the door and looked out. 'Where's that woman got to?'

'How did she go?'

'In the car, of course.'

'You have a car as well? Who drives what?'

'I drive this. I've got a heavy goods licence. I had a boy friend who had a haulage business. That's how it came about. All questions answered by return.'

'When did she go?'

'Oh, about nine. Something had got into her. I don't know what but she was hard black last night when we got back here. Hard black mood, that is. Dark, angry; storm-lulling in progress.'

'And this morning?'

'Short, sharp, steely. I left her alone. I read my book. Have you read Rabelais? Gargantua? Very rude, very funny, but so inventive. The language. I suppose that's the translator. Like Fitzgerald. He made Omar jolly. You wonder at my choice? My mother's a writer. She writes cookery books.'

'Interesting. Your father?'

'Retired Colonel. Busy with ideas for turning old pillboxes, foogooes and underground lavatories into fallout shelters. Breeds dogs. The place at home is all dogs. Everything's draped in Irish Setters. All right in hot weather. You get fanned by forty great wagging tails. Cold in winter, though.'

'Does your father travel about looking for these suitable dugouts?'

'Well, over certain areas. He has his favourite places. A girl in every foxhole, for all I know. Where the hell is she?'

'When's she due back?'

'She said eleven. To go riding. What's it now? Twelve?'

'Twenty minutes short.'

'She's usually punctual. That's what bothers. I don't know whether to shoehorn my bottom into my jodhpurs or not. I don't want to do that for nothing. You know, I could get away with riding if I rode side-saddle with a great long skirt and top hat. I might look graceful, even. Damn the woman!'

'What made you team up?' I said, as she drank some beer.

'Actually, it's my caravan, but I can't afford it so I rent it out with myself as well—driver, that is, and not with chaps, because that would be a bit call-girlish, and I haven't patience enough to be a whore.'

She was certainly plain spoken, I thought.

'Then I got a bit hooked on this psychic stuff,' she went on, 'and so I threw in my services as companion to the medium. I thought I might get a book out of it. As it happens, I got very involved seeing other people get sort of drugged with it. People who don't really need any help. People who can afford to pay don't need help. They need correction.'

'You are a surprising girl,' I said.

'No. I'm just a philosophical fattie.' She went to the door and looked out for a minute or more. Then she turned back. 'I don't know whether it's all this psychic kicking my nerves and sharpening up the old fear screens, but I have an awful heavy, draggy sort of feeling that something's happened to her.'

'Tell me what. You have some picture in your mind of what might have happened.'

'I always start with a road accident, but if that's right, then it was organised.' She looked at me very straight, as if to challenge me.

'What made you think that? Have you heard any threats?'

She looked away and frowned.

'I wasn't too keen on that place last night,' she said.

'Had you been there before?'

'No.'

'Then what made you feel uneasy?'

'That old mockery send-up; intuition. Spiritually speaking, there was a funny smell in the air. Like spiritual skunks.'

'Anyone particularly?'

'Bernard. I don't like Bernard.'

'He cultivates dislikes. It's quite deliberate. It means that if you want to do business with him, there's no friendship. It makes for clearer deals, he says.'

'There was the Magda woman, but she's an investigative journalist. It's a fancy name for what used to be done over garden fences and behind lace curtains, only now they do it by sorting out the insides of dustbins.'

'You are curiously forthright, Alice.'

'My dear Papa says I'll get myself murdered. Well, that's Bernard and Madga—Ball, or Bull, or whatever he says he is.' She nodded as if she had just realised something. 'That's the one. Not because he offered me fifty quid, understand—'

'When? Last night?'

'He said he liked fat girls. So I said I'd wait in his room and let Maria go home alone. I hope he waited. I didn't.'

'But that didn't make you spiritually uneasy?'

'Of course not. That made me laugh. But there's something about that man which makes me crawl inside. I don't know what it is, but I know it isn't physical.'

'You think he's up to something?'

'I think he's in with Bernard over something.' She sat down, staring at the doorway, so her eyes lit with the sunlight. 'Sometimes, when I meet people, I get a sudden mental picture of something. Ball gave me one last night. I had a short sharp impression that he could murder me—or anybody else—and not notice because he would be still thinking about himself.'

'You could be right,' I said. 'And Bernard?'

'I thought I had Bernard clear in my mind. He's just hard and selfish, and nobody else counts. But just now—coming here and snapping about like some snotty little suburban householder shooing you off a right of way—it wasn't his style. Do you think?'

'I was surprised.'

Somewhere beyond the trees the sound of a clock striking came softly in the quiet morning.

Alice got up.

'Something has happened!' she said, very sharply. 'I'm going to take a look.'

She went along the room and through a door. 'Excuse!' she called as the door fell to, and then through the panels I heard, 'Don't go!'

I put my glass down and went out of the caravan. Standing a few yards away from it I looked all round; at the trees of Bernard's wood, then across the gorse and little thorn trees in a sea of new bracken, until I came to the trees behind the caravan, then round across the track on which the van had come from the road and so back to the fringe of

Bernard's wood again.

What could he be so eager to defend? I could see nothing which could have interested his moneymaking sensibilities.

Yet he had fussed. He had been angry. The van had been parked there over a week, but he had not known until now, and he had been angry—or scared—enough to walk from the house, two miles I had reckoned on my trip, and kick up a fuss—not with caravanning strangers, but with someone he had invited into the area.

Had he suddenly found out they were there? If so, someone had told him, I thought. Then, knowing him and his tendency to listen to nobody unless he wanted an answer to a question put by himself, I reckoned he must have asked.

Or possibly he might have asked someone to see where I went for my walk, and then, if he had heard of the direction I had taken, he had probably used his Land-Rover up to the edge of the wood and then walked through.

All of which would have meant he had been in a hurry.

So what was important about this common land?

The girl had mentioned shadow factories of nearly forty years before. They had meant, according to records, purchase of lands by the Government for building factories, airfields, storage dumps and other necessities of war;

and some of the lands compulsorily bought had never been returned.

Was this common such a place? If so for what had it ever been used? There was no trace of bits of buildings that I could see.

I walked a little way along the track back to the road. It was, like so many tracks, two channels which the wheels of many vehicles had made leaving a grassy centre. The bottoms of the wheel channels were mostly hard, dry mud and squashed grass, but just a little way along I found something else. Over a distance of about three feet there were bits of old broken tarmac.

So once there had been a metalled track in through that gate from the road.

Something had once been there which had enjoyed the benefit of a small tarmac road, which from disuse had crumbled and been mostly covered by earth, grass and mud.

I looked back at the ground past the caravan, and at the trees to the right of it. But then Alice, in white shirt and blue slacks, came quickly towards me on her way to look for Maria.

'Are you coming?' she said.

'I should get back to lunch,' I said. 'I am Bernard's guest.'

'Yes, I suppose you are. 'Bye.'

She walked off fast towards the gate.

2

I walked around the common for twenty minutes, looking amongst gorse, bracken, peering around knolls and little dells but nowhere did I see any remnants of brick, concrete or any other sign that a building had once been there.

By that time I had to turn and head back to the house. The trees which had grown up by the once-metalled track had probably seeded from Bernard's wood years ago. Years, in fact, before Bernard had made the money which had finally enabled him to buy the place, only four years before.

As I walked back towards the house I thought about two loaded articulated trucks being hidden somewhere in the area, but so far I had found no possible hiding place for such vehicles.

At lunch Bernard asked me if I had enjoyed my walk. He asked with the intention of finding out where I had been.

I said I had been partly lost and wasn't sure. I mentioned, in passing, that I had an appointment that afternoon and might not be back before dinner.

'An old friend I haven't seen for years,' I said. 'A surveyor.'

'Oh, you were a surveyor, weren't you, Jonathan?'

'Yes.'

'Why did you stop?' said Magda.

'I wanted to do something else,' I said, and smiled.

'I'd like the choice,' grumbled Ball. He filled his fat mouth with fish and then literally washed it down his gullet with a great gulp of Moselle. He had the eating habits of a wild dog who gulps it all down until he chokes, in fear some other animal might want a bite. It was as if he didn't want to eat but did it to keep his boilers stoked.

In fact, I thought he was a sorely worried man. I comforted myself with the thought that perhaps he had sold a gun to a man who had threatened to blow his head off with it.

Then I realised that the idea proved that I, myself, was an unpleasant character.

'We shall try Maria again this evening,' Bernard said with a cold smile. 'I'm sure you'd all like to try again.'

'Of course,' Magda said, watching him steadily.

'I'm flying off tonight,' said Ball, washing down more fish.

'I have altered that to tomorrow,' said Bernard calmly, as if Ball was a little wooden chess piece to be moved around as he fancied.

Ball's gulp of Moselle almost choked him then. His face went almost purple, but after a grim struggle for air, he managed, like the snake with the rabbit, to get the mass of food down.

'I thought you was going to burst,' said Magda, with quiet interest. 'I was going to get up quick.'

Ball got up, threw his crumpled napkin on to the seat of his chair and strode out, leaving his lunch half-eaten.

'He'll probably take you by the throat if you say any more things like that,' said Bernard. 'Remember he is used to eating with all sorts of foreigners and such a lot of them eat like mechanical shovels. It can be catching. I know.'

So, having humiliated the absent Ball, Bernard mildly excused his gluttony, which made humiliation more complete somehow.

At that point I began to realise that my emotions were waking up to this whole situation, and that was a bad thing. I felt glad I had decided to go out alone that afternoon.

I drove off in the direction of the town, but no vehicle was on the road but mine, so I turned north up a minor road until I came to the gate between the woods where the caravan was. I parked across the gate, which was the only way not to obstruct the road too much, climbed over and went up to the caravan.

Alice was sitting on the top step, her arms resting on her knees, her chin on the top forearm. She swivelled her eyes to see me, but didn't raise her head.

'Is she back?' I said, halting.

Alice shook her head.

'I've got a car. We can look farther.'

'Yeap,' she said and got up. 'Yeap indeed.' She turned.

We drove northwards along the road until we came to a junction, where the main part of the road bent right and a smaller lane went straight on. I slowed down.

'Which way did you go?' I said.

'Round to the right.'

'We'll try straight on.'

The lane ran along the edge of the common, winding quite a lot and we passed another clump of trees which thickened into a wood. There was another five-bar gate and a track beyond like the one where the caravan was parked. I glanced aside to it then looked ahead as Alice squeaked.

'Look out! It's her!'

A car came round the bend ahead straight at us, then pulled off on to the grass verge and stopped. I stopped as we came alongside.

'Where have you been?' Alice shouted across me.

Maria looked out of the other car not at Alice, but at me, and her eyes glowed with what I thought could only be hatred. Her jaw was set tight, and she gripped the steering wheel as if trying to break it.

'Oh lord! She's in a spasm!' Alice said almost under her breath, and got out.

Alice went round to the other car.

'Take it easy, now,' she said. 'Let me drive.'

'What are you doing with that man!' Maria said bitterly.

'Trying to find you. Now ease off, Mar. Don't get all screwed up. Move over. You need rest.'

'Rest? How can I rest? I'm going back there tonight! I can't rest till afterwards. You know that, Alice! Oh, Alice—!'

As Alice opened the door Maria almost fell into her arms and sobbed very quietly. I drove on a little way and waited.

Like Alice, I wondered where Maria had been to get into such a state, and the way she had looked at me and said, *'that man'* made me think that, wherever she had been, she had found out about Randers' last encounter.

But how could she? No one had been with us that night and no one knew what had really happened then except the top-secret people to whom I had told the story.

The whole thing had been boiled down into a gun accident, and that had been that. There was no way Maria could have found out.

Unless she was truly psychic and could see through the veils of the years back to the scene that night, which was not credible to me, or, I thought, to anybody else.

Alice suddenly called out, 'Okay! See you this evening!' I turned and saw her get into the car and drive away.

I drove on along the track which made a sudden turn and went along the edge of an old quarry. I stopped and got out. The quarry, little more than a great hollow, had long filled with water below and bushes had taken root and grown on the rocky slopes of the crater. I drove further along till the track turned away from the quarry edge and joined a steep sloping cut which had once taken stone lorries down to the floor of the quarry. The road down was surfaced with broken stone through which grass had grown in places. On either side of the cut the slopes were steep, but even so, bushes and other vegetation had taken root.

I turned the car and drove away down the slope almost to the water's edge. Everything I saw looked like an innocent case of industrial activity gone to rot.

Somehow I felt it had such possibilities for what I had in mind, though I could see no useful sign of any recent visits there.

I backed up to the track again, turned and followed it down the way that lorries had once used. It was a rough road, strewn with potholes patched with bits of small broken stone from the quarry. It entered a wood of somewhat aged trees which were being strangled with ivy. The wood was fenced by old wood props and rusted barbed wire, some of which had fallen away from the posts. I slowed down as I saw a notice board just inside the wire. It was old and not much of the paint remained but I made out parts of the warning notice.

It appeared to warn loaded trucks to turn left, though the gate by which they had once come out of the wood was of iron and half buried in overgrowth.

If lorries had gone into such a place to load then the load had to be ammunition.

I felt I was getting very warm then, except for the fact that the gate and the fence had not been disturbed for many years. There is no value in finding a hiding place for two articulated trucks if there is no way the vehicles could have been got into such a place after 1950.

I drove on to where the track joined a road, and finally found my way round to the house again.

3

The scene in the séance room was as the night before, except for Magda's dress, which had been changed for one of greater cover. Ball had recovered his normal sullen composure, but Bernard was rather taut, even fidgety, and talked very little. He seemed to me to be angry, probably over something which he could not reach, because that always made him very angry indeed. In which case he wasn't angry about anyone in the house that night; nor the staff at his offices, for he could have blasted them over the phone hard enough to salve his itch.

An idea came to me which had been ghostly in my mind since Charles had set me on this track: Had Bernard someone above him in any enterprise?

That really was the question I most wanted to get an answer to.

We waited. The quiet conversation was sparse. Suddenly Bernard sat back.

'Where is the bloody woman?' he said, very angry then.

'She did come?' said Magda.

'Of course she came!' Bernard snapped. 'Of course she came. My chauffeur brought her. He reported the fact to me more than half an hour ago!'

'You must not rush these people,' I said, deliberately sticking a goad into his anger.

He looked at me. I saw in his face all the fury of a frustrated hate for me. It was no surprise. We had never had any affection for each other, but his emotion then was something to take careful note of.

The door opened behind him, but it was Alice, not Maria, who came in.

'She's not well,' said Alice, looking round the faces at the table. 'You must wait a little longer.'

'Tell her to come in!' said Bernard, without looking at the girl. 'Tell her to come in!'

'No,' said Alice, and turned to go. 'She needs time.'

CHAPTER FIVE

1

Alice appeared to smile to herself and walked out. Bernard almost snorted with rage and frustration. At that party he was showing far too much rage and nostril-flaring.

I guessed his nerves were in almost as bad a state as Ball's, but he had a different way of showing the symptoms. He was so used to shouting at people anyhow that an unusual amount of shout was not immediately apparent.

'Jonathan, you know the woman!' he said sharply. 'Go and see if you can persuade her, there's a good chap. You're a diplomat, when you feel like it.'

'Tell her she won't get her fee,' said Magda, calmly. 'It usually works.'

'I doubt it,' I said, and got up.

I wanted to go, to satisfy my own curiosity. Maria had been very strange that day, and I wanted to get an idea why she had pointed at me as at an enemy when we had met her in the car.

Alice had looked surprised at it, so she hadn't known of this attitude either. I still didn't think she could have found out what actually did happen to Randers, but I felt uneasy.

My knock at the dressing-room door was answered by Alice, who opened it looked out at me then turned without closing the gap.

'It's Mr Blake,' she said. 'He's all right, isn't he?'

I didn't hear the answer but Alice turned back to me and opened the door wide.

'Come on in. It's Smelling Salts Hour.'

Maria was lying on the sofa staring at the wall beyond her feet.

'What the hell do you want?' she said, without looking round.

'Bernard sent me to find out if you'll do it or not,' I told her. 'I said you'd please yourself, anyway.'

'Too right,' she said, still without looking round. 'But I'm scared.'

'Of what? Can I help?'

'No. The voice last night. Mostly, when I am in touch, I am somehow aware of what is going on, though it's hazy and faraway. I don't know exactly what is said through me, but often the gist comes to me, even if it's afterwards. But last night there was nothing at all.'

'What happened after you sat down last night?'

'I suddenly came over sleepy and very vague. I closed my eyes to shake off the feeling, but I must have fallen asleep! It doesn't seem possible, but I went to sleep for a minute or maybe much more. I don't know.

But I don't want that again.'

'You're frightened of what you might say?'

'After what happened last night—yes. Everybody round the table recognised that voice. But I can't do voices like that. I'm not an imitator or a mimic. What I say I have to say in my own voice. People tell me that, but how could it be otherwise? I'm not a performer. I can't take people off.'

I looked round the room and saw two small bottles of ginger ale on a tray with one glass.

'Let me help,' I said.

I went to the tray, made sure the glass was clean, then took a small flask from my pocket and poured her a Scotch.

'Do you always carry that?' she said as I took her the short drink.

'My mother wanted me to be a good Samaritan. This was the only equipment I could think of.'

She watched me as she drank.

'You don't think it'll happen again, do you?'

'Not if you swallow that and just come straight in after me.' I went to the door. 'Right?'

Alice said, 'He's got it taped, Mar. Do what he says.'

Maria got up.

They were still sitting around the table. Bernard looked round sharply as I came in.

'She said she's coming now,' I said.

'I knew you'd manage it,' Bernard said, with

a trace of acid. 'Sit down. We must get composed.'

We sat round the lamp. Maria came in very soon after. She sat down in her chair. We spread our hands on the table, fingers touching. Bernard stamped the light out at the foot switch. It was then pitch dark.

Once again I sensed a tension in the air, as if uneasiness spread fast amongst the sitters. I felt Magda's finger tremble slightly against mine. Ball, I think, made little hissing noises as if whispering some kind of toneless tune. He stopped. The silence came again. I could feel a greater tension building up all round me. I had an odd feeling that somebody would scream.

If they did I thought it would be because one of the others had stabbed in the dark and struck home. By the time the lights came on again each would be back in his proper place. I realised I was mentally assuming that Magda would be stabbed.

Why?

Ball began to hiss sharply again as if the strain was getting too much for his boiler pressure. Again his hiss stopped short.

The tension in the air was becoming unbearable. I felt that someone must get up and break the circle. By then I could hear Magda's breathing.

There was no sound from Maria at all.

We were all waiting on her, but nothing happened. I heard small restless movements;

70

people shifting on their seats, moving their feet uneasily on the carpets. Someone coughed in a muffled, half-frightened sort of way.

I imagined Bernard getting more and more frustrated and angry about this protracted, useless wait in the darkness.

Then gradually, I made out a lighter shade in the black somewhere behind Maria's chair. It was so faint and indistinct I was not sure, at first, if it was there.

'Someone is appearing!' Magda spoke in German in a voice so small and tight that it was almost inaudible.

No one at the table answered. I felt Maria's finger working against mine as if some kind of tiny paroxysm was passing through her muscles.

The shade of brighter light became more distinct; a green misty patch in the dark. It seemed to have depth, like a vague, luminous goldfish bowl.

I heard someone breathing hard, then there was silence again.

'Bloody hell!'

The swearing came from Maria. Her hand was snatched from the table beside mine. Bernard said something; Ball muttered; Magda leant against my arm and I felt her shudder.

'Whatever this green thing is, it's nothing to do with me!' Maria cried, very firmly indeed. 'It isn't a spirit. It's a fake!'

'Lights!' Magda called out.

'Okay! Okay!' Bernard snapped out the words but seemed to be fumbling with his feet. 'It doesn't work! The switch doesn't work!'

'I'll do the main ones,' Ball said.

We heard him stumbling about, crashing into furniture, calling out, 'Where the hell's the door?'

Then he obviously thumped into it and heavy though it was it rattled uneasily from the impact.

'Switch it on!' Bernard said angrily.

'It doesn't work!' Ball said in exasperated tones.

We heard him snapping the switch up and down. 'Your power's gone!'

I got up, keeping the position of Maria's chair-back in my mind's eye and as I moved to one side I reached out and touched it. I felt her hair under my wrist.

'Sit still,' I said.

The greenish glow was still suspended in the middle of the blackness a few feet behind the chair. I still could not make out what it was though by then I was quite near to where it had to be, unless it was shining through the wall.

I heard Ball open the room door. No light came from outside.

'Why the hell hasn't Barker done something?' Bernard said, very angrily indeed. He began to shout. 'Barker! Barker! Where's the bloody bell-push?'

It seemed I was the only one still interested in the luminous patch in the darkness.

I came to a point where I believed it was very near. I reached out carefully and my hand went flat against the wall. As I did that, the glow vanished.

I heard Magda start to say, 'Look! He's—'

At that moment the lights came on. After a darkness so intense the first few seconds of light were a blinding glare, for owing to the snapping of the switches every light in the room came on.

I closed my eyes a moment to ease the glare, then looked at the patch of wallpaper under my hand as I lifted it. It was old paper, and there was a patch of faded colour on it as if something had seeped through from behind. I looked round for a moment. Maria was twisted in her chair, watching me. Bernard was at the door, turned towards me. Ball had gone. Magda sat at the table holding a hand over her eyes. 'There's a hole behind here,' I said, and turned away.

'Is there?' Bernard said. 'I'll have it filled in. I'm sorry, Maria. Everything was spoilt.'

'It doesn't matter. The atmosphere is wrong,' she said, and got up.

'Wrong? But you've sat here before!'

'It was wrong last night. Someone is wrong here. It doesn't work with them. I've tried, but one person blocks it.'

Bernard went towards her slowly. Magda was watching Maria intently. Bernard stopped by the high-backed chair. Behind him Ball came in through the door, looked towards the table and halted, holding the door edge.

'How can one person block it, Maria?' said Bernard, slowly, almost icily.

'You know that if death is present, no contact can be made.'

'Death?' said Bernard, in a strained voice. 'Do you mean one of us?'

'Yes.'

'What's she mean?' Ball demanded, as if angered by the suggestion.

'One of you here tonight is near to death,' Maria said, and got up from the chair. 'Very near. So near that it works as a bar against any spirit wanting to contact us.'

'Who?' said Ball, eyes bulging. *'Who!'*

Maria walked round the table towards the door.

'I can't tell,' she said. 'I can feel it, but it's in the group. Which one it is, I couldn't tell. But it's certainly there.'

For a moment Ball, in his extreme alarm, looked as if he would stop her going out in order to make her tell what she didn't know, but he stood back at the last moment, and she left the room.

'How did a light come through the wallpaper?' Bernard said. 'It's never done it before!'

'Are you sure?' I said.

He hesitated.

'Of course I'm not. I'm not here all the time.'

'Damn that!' said Ball. 'What about this death business? Is she genuine, that girl? I mean—could she know?'

'Mediums and seers—yes, they know,' Bernard said. 'They don't see the future. They *feel* it. They feel it coming. My mother was very well into the psychic world—'

'You're talking as if it isn't you!' Ball said.

'I don't think it is,' Bernard said. 'But none of us can be sure.' He looked straight into Ball's face. 'Can we?'

He walked out.

'He is a boor,' said Magda, and taking equipment from her small evening bag she began to survey her face and then make minor adjustments to her decoration.

'How can she know?' said Ball, looking from Magda to me as if for help.

'She knows that one of us tonight is going to die,' said Madga, pulling weird mouths as she lipsticked. 'That is what she said. Who is most likely? Do you have indigestion a lot, Mr Ball? Or do your cheeks always puff and blow and glow like that?'

'Don't be a fool, Magda!' Bernard shouted from the corridor. 'Come here to me, please! Here!'

With a curious look at me, Magda picked up her bag and walked out. I crossed the room.

Ball was talking to himself, it seemed.

'Rubbish. Utter, bloody rubbish! How can anybody know?'

'One person could,' I said.

'Who? Who could know?'

'A would-be murderer,' I said. 'Go over your friends in your mind. If nobody's sharpening a knife, you're in the clear.'

I went out and left him. I saw him go to the drinks table as I turned to go down the corridor.

The corridor was empty. I went to the next door along from the séance room, opened the door, went in, and closed the door behind me.

It was a sort of games-and-gun room. Rackets, golf clubs, a variety of shoes suitable for various pastimes were arranged on shelves round the walls. The right-hand wall was all cupboards. I opened the first and saw a range of sporting guns in their racks, and on the wall at the back was a scribble in indelible pencil.

J. Green, Cpl,
ROC 1942

The initials stood for both Royal Observer Corps, and Royal Ordnance Corps, at the time of the writing.

Two miles away, due north, I had found the old entrance to an ammunition loading base, so I had to assume that the initials stood for the Royal Ordnance Corps, Masters of Shot and Shell.

It began to look as if, more than forty years ago, the place had been taken over as a military HQ which controlled a considerable store of guns, ammunition and other gruesome necessities of war.

Many of these, I knew from records I had seen, had been underground stores, and like a lot of other things which multiplied and yet grew less in the vaults of the Government Files, some records had been lost over the years.

I stood back and looked up. The cupboards reached to the ceiling. Government departments always have lots of room for everything. I remembered once seeing an official safe opened by two officials, each with his own key, the two keys having to work together. Inside the safe was a single file containing one sheet of paper which contained the numbers of ten other files which should be consulted.

The middle cupboard was locked when I tried it, so was the end one.

The light which had shone through the wallpaper must have come from somewhere at the back of the cupboard.

Moreover the light had shone when the house power had been cut off.

I left the room carefully, making sure the corridor was empty before I stepped out and closed the door behind me. I went along to the hall, and out on to the front steps. It was a fine, warm night. I went down to the drive and strolled along to where the cars were parked. In my car I hinged up the ashtray between the front seats, unlocked the plate under it with a special key and lifted the lid. I took out my .38 revolver, a small box of ammunition, and replaced them with the silver whisky flask before I locked up the small compartment and swung the ashtray back into place.

The social part of the visit might be about to come to a sudden end and I had to be prepared for it.

3

At 2 a.m. the house was silent. I put on loose-cut cords that didn't show any untoward bulges in the pockets, a shirt and a roll-neck jersey. Soft-soled shoes ensured a quiet passage. A torch, a gun and an all-purpose penknife completed the outfit.

I knew that if Bernard came out and spotted me I should be clobbered. He would naturally think I was meaning to burgle his secret business deals to make money for myself. That would be very unpopular indeed with him.

The other person I had to watch out for was the chauffeur. Large, silent, almost merging into any background he fronted, he seemed the perfect watchdog.

I heard nothing on my way down to the hall, but at the bottom of the stairs I stopped and listened again. A clock ticked seconds quietly, and that was the only sound in the sleeping palace.

I went along and shut myself in the gun room. My examination of the cupboard fronts was careful, and with the gadget on my all-purpose penknife I opened the lock of the centre cupboard without trouble.

Inside there was a flight of wooden steps going down on to a concrete floor. At one side a notice was stuck to the wall, warning all personnel that regulation service boots were forbidden and shoes, rubber, only were to be worn.

The wall ahead of the stairs as they went down had two bricks missing, which explained the 'ghost light' in the séance room. But it had also shone so steadily I did not think it had been someone holding a torch.

There was a lamp hanging over my head with an old brass switch on the cupboard wall. When I snapped the switch the light came on, but it was very low-powered. I turned it off again and used the torch only to go down to the bottom of the flight. Shining the light round showed only part of an old wine cellar.

Some of the bottle racks were piled up against a brick wall on the left.

The place was all niches and alcoves formed by brick arches supporting the house walls above. There were a few old crates and boxes lying about, but no sign that the place had been used for years. Perhaps all those years ago there had been an ammunition store down there, which accounted for the notice above, but it wasn't the sort of place I was looking for.

I knew what it would extend to: a corridor to the boiler room, store room, fuel store, all as much alike as this vault to the next vault along.

Yet that evening somebody had been here, and the light at the top of the stairs had not needed the main supply to the house.

I think it was that which persuaded me to keep on looking.

Now and again, as I went deeper into the vaults I stopped and listened. More than once the Silent Chauffeur came into my mind as I listened for a sound of anyone following in my footsteps. He, of all people, was the mute keeper of Bernard's secrets. He knew all about the séances with Maria, and I wished I did, but the last person I would ask would be that rock-faced driver.

There were shelves in some of the alcoves, of which there were eight, spanning the depth of the house. At the far end there were stone steps leading up to the door, which was the main way down from the kitchen end of the building.

I turned and began to go back, because somewhere I thought there might be another door which I had not seen.

I found it deep in an alcove where there was quite a stack of old crates and boxes and a couple of wine racks. They did not hide the door, but the shadow thrown by my torchlight did.

It was an old door, and hefty. There was a modern hasp and padlock on it. Again I used my all-purpose knife and opened the lock.

Beyond the door was an old brick tunnel. It was not the sort of tunnel I'd hoped to find, but clearly one of the old single ways to an earth room, probably under one of the lawns. Originally the rooms of this sort had been used for storing ice cut from the ponds in winter. The blocks had kept for months in these earth rooms.

For a moment I hesitated over wasting time going down the tunnel, but I was searching, so I went.

There was a bend in the tunnel, and round it, a steel door on the right-hand side, with half-obliterated notices of warning painted on it.

There was another padlock.

Clearly this had been the Commanding Officer's way through to whatever it was lay beyond the iron door.

That padlock was more difficult than the last and took two or three minutes. Three times, I think it was, I stopped to listen, disturbed by the slow sound of dripping water, and turned off the torch.

The feeling that somebody was there was very strong, and I waited in the darkness hoping that silence on my part would encourage any follower to think I had gone on ahead, and so would follow and come within my reach.

I had no illusion about what would happen otherwise.

If, as Charles had suspected, there was something big and unpleasant in hand, then it was sensible to expect several people to be involved.

And if one of the prizes was a couple of truckloads of bullion, then anybody interfering, like myself, would be treated summarily; with a bullet, or several.

That expectation was what held me to a certain caution in this nocturnal expedition. If I were murdered in the ice tunnel only the murderers would know, because the world would be given to understand I had skipped with very valuable business information which I had intended to sell.

I had seen Bernard's sort of work before and his handling of people's reputations always made them very black indeed, so the public would believe it with pleasure.

Charles wouldn't start police enquiries. He was a philosopher. If I got lost, very sad. He would get somebody else.

I shielded the torch when I switched it on again by putting it inside my jersey. I got the padlock open.

The water kept dripping, very slowly and irregularly. I listened to it intently and put the smothered light out.

In the darkness I unhooked the padlock, swung open the hasp and grasped the grip handle of the steel door.

Then I heard a small stone fall. It came from somewhere round the bend of the tunnel, between the bend and the vaults.

CHAPTER SIX

1

I knew that someone was behind me, and so, between me and the only way out I knew. By the way he was moving so quietly and carefully I guessed he meant to collar me first and then raise an alarm afterwards.

Just how many people were engaged in this secret organisation I could not guess, but it had to be quite a number, so that even if he failed to overcome me by his surprise tactics, there could be no doubt he had the means on him to blow the whistle on my hoped-for escape.

I guessed that he would think I was at the door and backed away from it further up the tunnel, moving without making any sound. About three paces from the door I stopped and listened.

There was a slow drip of water from somewhere behind me; obviously water seeping through the old brick roof of the tunnel.

The darkness was absolute and the quiet as stifling as a tomb. The occasional soft drip of water seeming to accentuate the silence.

Then I heard a faint sound as of the padlock being moved on its hasp, and then saw something very foolish, but which was lucky for me.

By the edge of the door, where I knew the padlock to be, I saw the luminous green circle of a wristwatch dial. From that I knew roughly where the man's legs had to be and I went forward as quietly as I had gone away. I got the wrist just above the glow of the watch face, jerked the arm across me and at the same time kicked in the direction I knew the legs would be. It was an old judo throw I learnt years ago, but which usually depends on being able to see.

In this case it didn't matter that much because the tunnel was so narrow that as soon as the man went headlong across me some part—I think the skull—hit the brickwork with what has been called a sickening thud. On the moment of that thud his wrist was wrenched out of my grip because the whole of him went down across my feet and stayed there.

I made sure that he was out and likely to stay so for a short time and then made my way back through the cellar and up into the old ordnance office. I closed the cupboard door there, left everything as I had found it, then went upstairs to my bedroom.

Sometimes one has an instinctive sense of some presence that shouldn't be there. I had one such as I grasped the door handle, and hesitated as a result.

But commonsense told me that anyone waiting in the room for me must have heard the small rattle of the door handle being grasped, so I opened the door and went in.

The table light was on. Ball was standing by it, fully dressed, but looking as if someone had yanked him along by his tie. He turned his head as I went in and watched me close the door behind me.

'What are you doing in here?' I said.

'Waiting for you.'

'I've been out to get some air. This place is stuffy.' I sat on the end of the bed. 'Why did you wait for me?'

'I'm getting out.'

'What do I care about that?'

'I've got the tickets. What I need is a guarantee I can get to use them.'

'From me? What kind of guarantee have I got to give? Who do you think I am?'

'I know who you are. At the moment you're on a very sticky wicket, but you can get out of it, because you've got some heavy guns you can call up when you need them.'

'I think you've got the wrong man. But tell me what sort of guarantee you imagine I can give.'

'You can hamstring Bernard.'

'You mean I can stop him from stopping you getting away and disappearing?'

'I mean that.'

'Why do you think that?'

'You're the only one here he's scared of. I can read that off clearly enough. If you told him to lay off for a while, he'd lay off.'

'I think you're in a pipe-dream, Ball. I can't stop him doing what he wants. In any case, didn't he say you're flying off in the morning? So what's the trouble?'

'I won't get near any fly-off if you don't hold him back.'

It began to dawn on me that he thought I was something that I wasn't. It was true that Bernard had always been wary of me, but perhaps he had his own reasons for that, and I didn't know them. But Ball had to have some very peculiar and very strong reason for thinking I could just give a signal and Bernard would do as he was told.

'I want to know more,' I said. 'I want to know why you want to get out now.'

'If I don't, I don't go anywhere any more.'

'I see. Where did you slip up?'

'The girl. The bloody fortune-teller. That's what she's here for. To get the line on everybody and report to Bernard.'

'You've been to these séances before?'

'Once.'

'You don't mean you believe she can see through anybody there, do you?'

'No, I think she's just an investigator. He gives her the name. She finds out.'

'I repeat my question: Where did you slip up?'

'I don't know. I know I was on the skids when he told me he'd altered my flight. That's a sure sign you've lost control when he starts altering your arrangements.'

'That seems a long guess to me. He might have just wanted you to stay a few hours longer.' I shrugged to make my following question look unimportant. 'What do you do for him, anyway?'

'I have many contacts. He makes use of them when he finds one useful to him.' He was evasive, but I felt I wasn't going to get any more out of him about Bernard than that.

He still thought he could get away with it alive, I supposed.

'So what this meeting boils down to is that you want to go and you don't want Bernard to have you followed?'

'Just that.'

'But you're wrong about my influence. I couldn't stop him doing what he wants.'

He stared at me.

'But you're in it, aren't you?' he said, and for the first time he looked as if he might have made a bad mistake.

'Why in hell do you think I'd tell you, one way or another?'

He turned away, and looked as if he realised that his last hope had gone. The muscles of his back relaxed as if they no longer wanted to hold his head up.

New hope braced him suddenly and he turned back to me.

'You were with Randers in Berlin?' he said.

'I looked for him there—once.'

'There you knew what he was after?'

'No. I wanted to find out. Anyhow, it was years ago.'

'In a case like this years don't make any difference.'

I looked at him.

'Meaning it takes years to get it together? But this was a long time back.'

'It takes all that. Damn it! You should know!'

'I haven't been around all the time. My business with Randers was something which ended around the same time that he did. I knew he was up to something else but it didn't interest me then.'

'And yesterday we are entertained with a track of his voice saved from all those years ago. Why? He died. We all knew that. But I was there when he spoke those words about the man who had come to know—to find out.'

'Who was it?'

'He didn't know the man's real name. He called him "Conquest".'

'Well, if that tape was dug up for last night, Bernard might think that Conquest is still here.'

'Or has just arrived here,' Ball said. 'And if he has—' he broke off.

'If he has, that's your reason for wanting to leave without trace?'

'My reason for wanting to go is Bernard.

You can hold Bernard back from getting after me. That's what I ask. In return I've told you I'm sure Conquest is either here now, or will be within a few hours.' He went to the door.

'I haven't promised anything,' I said.

'Hold him off me. Do that and I'll promise to let you know everything about Conquest in twenty-four hours. I know exactly where to find it. You promise your part, I promise to send you mine. Once you've got it, I shall be safe anyway. It's the twenty-four hours I need from you.'

'You should have said that to start with.'

'I didn't know how to take you.'

'And how do I get this message? It can't be sent here.'

'You ought to get out of here. But if you won't, I'll get a phone call put through. It won't be me talking. The person who does the talking won't know what the message means. But you will.'

He stared at me for a moment.

'Okay?' he said.

'I agree to do what I can for you.'

He nodded, opened the door and went out, closing it very quietly behind him.

There was an interval of, I suppose three seconds before I heard the soft spit of a silenced gun. I went to the door, opened it very quietly about an inch and peered through the gap towards the head of the stairs.

Ball was lying there on the rich carpet, half

on his side, face towards me as if he had turned too late to see something that had been behind him.

The bullet hole in his forehead showed he had been a lot too late.

I closed the door again but opened it a second later just a half-inch at most. I saw a shadow approaching the dead man on the staircarpet.

I stayed watching. I wanted to see who was going to do the clearing up.

2

The affair was carried out in silence. Two men in slacks and tee shirts appeared and put a rolled-up stretcher by the deceased. In a second, the stretcher was unrolled and Ball was on it. A third man appeared, wearing a lounge suit. He tossed a rug over the corpse and the two men carried the covered stretcher silently down the stairs.

The remaining man sprayed the carpet with some sort of stain remover, left it several seconds, then produced a small brush from his pocket, brushed the carpet where Ball had left a little blood, then went away down stairs.

None of the three ever looked towards my door. None needed to. They knew where Ball had come from.

I closed the door. There was a possibility that the man who had tracked me from the cellar had thought me to have been Ball. In which case, I had no need to worry for a few hours.

I thought I might be overestimating by hoping for a little peace, but there was a mortice bolt on the door, so I shot that and went to bed. A little sleep is a worthy weapon against overstress.

And I felt there would be plenty such stresses starting the first thing next morning.

At breakfast, Bernard said, 'So he made his trip after all.'

'Who?' Magda said.

'Ball, of course. Silly ass. I could have put him on to some useful work if he'd stayed. Will you be all right for tonight, Jonathan? I have a special visitor on his way. Didn't hear till this morning. Damn feller always rings up around seven a.m. Uncivilised.'

'Not another séance?' I said, curiously.

'That woman's lost touch!' Bernard snapped. 'They do say these mediums can drift right away from their contacts in time. She's been a dead loss this trip, I'm afraid. Sorry. But how can one tell?'

The staff still seemed to be composed of the chauffeur, who doubled as steward-butler and commandant of the two women who came in from the village to clean. There was no sign of the gymnast stretcher-bearers of the previous night, nor the big man in the suit who had cleaned the spotted carpet so efficiently.

I had not seen any of their faces. They had merely passed my door, done their work and gone straight on downstairs.

My guess was that they were employed in the old underground ammunition storage base into which I had so nearly penetrated the previous night.

Bernard's manner was offhand, and yet still hard. I saw Magda look at him curiously while he was intent on buttering toast. He had already returned his breakfast half eaten and the toast buttering looked as if it was just something for Bernard to do without having to look at us.

I think that was the first time I'd thought that of Bernard. It gave me the feeling that he was not entirely in command of the general situation.

Suddenly he left the toast, got up and went out of the room. Magda looked at me with raised eyebrows.

'Something has gone wrong,' she said. 'Is it Ball going away when Bernard didn't want it?'

'It might be Ball,' I said. 'Certainly something's got up his nose.'

'I thought it would be a party,' Magda said, her voice quite low. 'But nobody came.'

'Perhaps somebody is coming now,' I said. 'That could be what he was talking about.'

'But he said only one. It seems like one at a time. We shall get no party from that. You know what, Mr Blake? I am getting bored with this. He does not seem to know exactly what he is doing. It's strange for a man like that.'

'It could be a deal has gone badly adrift. He always has a lot of money at risk.'

She shrugged.

'You take me out this morning,' she said, getting up. 'I wish to see something of this damn place. I am sick of the inside of it.'

'You didn't bring a car?' I said.

'Oh, no. He sent the chauffeur to the station for me. I don't use a car over here. I hire one with a driver when I need. The company pays, of course. It's very simple.'

She went up to her room. I was annoyed. I had hoped to find where Alice, Maria and the big caravan had gone, or even if it had taken Bernard's warning and left. I needed to keep a connection with the outside world in case it became neccessary to send a message in a hurry.

Sooner or later the mystery men of the body-clearance squad were going to get the message that Ball had not been down in the cellars, and when they did, my number would be up in Bernard's house. Bernard might hold them back for a bit once he knew, because he was now in an uncertain state of nerves and would probably think that I was not working for myself. That was a hope borne of Bernard's new—to me—nervousness and uncertainty which he kept showing.

At that time I knew so much, but did not

guess the rest. I thought then that the stolen bullion trucks had been hidden in the old officially forgotten underground ammunition dump.

That fact—if it was a fact—was not enough. Why hide the stuff for so long? Why stand the risk of discovery for so long? It made no sense.

Also, as I had seen following Ball's death, there was a hidden staff in this place which had nothing to do with household affairs. I guessed that they were attached to the underground establishment.

But they were obviously trained men, almost an Army stage of training had been shown in the rapid and certain disposal of that body from the stairs. Not a second had been wasted; not a trace had been left; not a sound had been made that I had heard but the faint hiss of the stain remover used by the big man.

But why trained men kept on their toes to guard almost forgotten bullion stolen years before? It made no sense.

But then nor did Charles's original proposition to me make sense. What did he care about stolen bullion? He had hoped it would lead to something much more savage than that. So had I. But in two days all I'd found was this old underground dump and the possibility that it was being used and closely guarded.

But for two bullion trucks? Rubbish! After all this time the cost of protection would have passed the profit likely to be made on a secret sale.

Then a coincidence struck. It wasn't great, but it was one.

Ball had spoken of a Big Shot due to appear soon whom he knew only as 'Conquest'.

Charles had told me that exhaustive research had turned up with an enigma by the name of 'Catkin'.

There was no resemblance between the words, but both began with 'C' and both indicated big names which weren't known.

Was it possible that Ball's 'Conquest' could be Charles's 'Catkin'?

Charles had added up a large total of bullion and art treasures, all stolen without signature as if engineered by a computer.

Ball had merely mentioned 'Conquest' as the name which Randers had given years before, because Randers, too, had never known a name but had known the man was Big.

If he was still Big those years after, then he was no criminal adventurer, but more likely a man in a big way of criminal business, employing, organising and planning for several expert thieves.

Whatever may be the general belief, most outstanding works of art filched in burglaries are recovered because they are so difficult to get rid of, and mad American millionaire collectors belong almost to a bygone age.

Magda came down into the hall. The

chauffeur/major domo was on his way upstairs and waited for her to pass him on the landing.

My car was standing to one side of the drive. We got into it. As I drove off down towards the road she switched on the radio. Then after a moment of music, pushed another button.

'I don't like Mozart in the morning,' she said. 'Some things do not belong to the morning.' She pushed a third button. 'Nor do I wish for a talk about babies in Peru—' she pushed again—'Hell! Wagner? What's Wagner doing at a time like this? Is there no light music in the wide world?' She pushed again.

A soft, regular bleeping came. She looked at me.

'What is that?'

I turned out into the road.

'It is a signal telling me that a bug has been stuck on my car,' I said, and switched the set off.

She stayed looking at me.

'Was it there yesterday?'

'No.'

She looked round through the rear window.

'This is bad. You are in trouble.'

I stopped the car.

'Stay there,' I said and took my small bug-detector from my pocket. The small light flicked steadily and grew brighter as I went towards the rear of the car. It gave a steady light by the rear wing. I reached under the lip and felt the small transmitter sticking like a magnet to the underside of the wing.

I got back in the car.

'You have got it?'

'I have found where it is,' I said, and drove on.

'You are leaving it?'

Instead of turning into the left-hand lane which led past the site of the big caravan, I kept straight on into the village.

Outside the Post Office and general store there was a small mail van opportunely parked.

'I want a paper,' I said, getting out. 'I won't be a moment.'

I passed the rear of the car, reached under the wing and unstuck the transmitter, then stuck it to the back end of the mail van as I went by to the shop. I went into the shop and bought a paper. The postman was just taking away the morning collection in a sack.

I paid for the paper, and when I went out the little red van was driving away merrily down the road.

We drove on through the village to the first left turn, and then I made my way through the winding lanes back to where the caravan had been.

'Where are we going?' Magda said.

'I want to see some friends,' I said.

When we reached the site, the van had gone. Bernard's warning had been taken to heart.

I turned right along the road towards the

disused quarry. When we came almost to the quarry edge I saw the van and its attendant car standing to the left of the road by the side of the old fenced wood.

Alice was outside the van in shorts and shirt, watching my car with interest.

'That girl was with the medium,' Magda said, without emotion.

'That's right,' I said. 'Just hang on. I want to find Maria if I can.'

I got out and went to Alice.

'You moved,' I said.

'Maria made me. She's dead scared of Bernard. I said, "He can't kill you if you don't" and she said, "Don't you be too sure of that, either". I think she's going off her head with all this psycho business. I don't think she's strong enough to play about with it like that. I had an aunt who went funny trying to get in touch with an old lover—'

'Very sad,' I said. 'But where is Maria now?'

'There was a phone call.'

'You've got a phone in the van?'

'I've got everything in the van.'

'So she got a call. Then what?'

'She said she'd got to meet a fellow with the money for the séances. Bernard was paying her off, she said.' Alice pointed towards the distant lane which led, as I knew, past the old forgotten entrance to the underground dump. 'She walked down there to meet him. I got on with the housework.'

99

CHAPTER SEVEN

1

I walked to the corner of the old Army lane and looked along past the one-time entrance. No one was there. I turned and looked down the long ramp to the flooded quarry. That, too, was bare of people.

If Maria had met anyone, then she had gone away with them.

When I got back to the caravan, Magda was out of the car and talking to Alice. The fair girl stared when I told her Maria had gone.

'But she wouldn't have gone off with anyone!' she said. 'We were leaving here.'

'And she just told you she was to meet someone to collect her fee and then go?' I said.

'That's what she said. She was on about the whole thing this morning, how it had been a failure and how mad Bernard was and all the rest of it. She was really upset. She wouldn't have gone with anybody else!'

'Then why didn't the man with the money come here?' I said. 'Why skulk round the corner where you wouldn't see him?'

'Don't ask me!' Alice said. 'Some things she was open about and others she would walk a mile to hide from you—' She watched me closely. 'You think something's happened, don't you?'

'I'm not sure. When you left the house last night was there any row between Maria and Bernard?'

'No. He was too ice cold to row. It almost made me think he really believed in her psychic power.'

'You doubt that he did?'

She shook her head.

'It's difficult to say with men like that, but I always had the idea that he used her to frighten his friends,' Alice said. 'People are very superstitious, and it always seems to me the bigger risks people take the worse they are.'

'Do you think that was the idea this time? Last night and the night before?' I said.

'Yes. But something went wrong. The person meant to be scared didn't take, I'd say. But I warn you, I'm a novelettish sort of guesser, as my father said.'

'As far as she was concerned, do you think she really believed she had this mediumistic gift?' I said.

'She's like the rest of us,' Alice said impatiently. 'She has ups and she has downs. When she's down she doubts. Don't we all?'

All this time Magda was listening and no doubt mentally recording with true interrogative instinct. I turned to her suddenly.

'What did you go to Bernard's to

investigate, Magda?'

She looked at me quickly.

'My magazine suggested I look at him. As a financier, that is,' she added.

'What about the séance angle?' I said.

'But of course. Like Hitler. He used to go by the spirits. Of course, it's easy to say it never works, but very often it does for a long time before it starts to go wrong. It did for Hitler. Maybe it has done for Bernard. But if now it's begun to go wrong—and it looked like it the last two nights—then he could be mad about it.'

'Was there no other angle you were interested in about Bernard?' I said.

She began to look defensive.

'What do you mean?'

'Randers is cold meat. Dead a long time,' I said, 'but all of a sudden he comes alive again. You knew him, and you turn up at Bernard's for the return celebrations. Ball knew him, too.'

'Ball has gone,' Magda said, with a slight touch of relief.

I took a risk then and it came off.

'Ball hasn't gone,' I said. 'He was shot dead last night at the top of the stairs and carried off by staff I've never seen before.'

Magda stared at me.

'Murdered?' she said, and then swore softly in German.

'Who did it?' Alice said. 'Bernard?'

102

'No. But I think it was done on his orders.'

'To stop him going?' Magda said.

'I don't think he ever had the chance of going. The visit to Bernard's was planned to be his last trip.' I looked from one to the other of them.

'Did you see it happen?' Alice said.

'Yes.'

'Why didn't you go to the police?'

'There was nothing to show them. Everything was cleared up.'

'So you're going to leave it, just like that?' Alice said.

I looked at her hard.

'What would you do?'

'Run,' she said, and shrugged. 'I wouldn't want a misfired shotgun at my back. These shooting accidents are so easy to get away with. Specially when the victim's an itinerant like me.'

'Magda, would you go to the police?' I said.

'No. I never mix with the police in foreign countries. One never knows how it might turn round on you.'

'Yes, it might do that,' I agreed. 'Just tell me this, Magda; did you come here because you'd heard about the resurrection of Randers?'

'There was talk in Dresden. About a month ago. I had a permit to cover an exhibition there. But it wasn't Randers who was spoken of, but his plan.'

'The Randers Plan?'

'That's what it seemed to be. As I'd known the villain, I was interested, if only because if he ever did have a plan he would have sold it to both sides at once.'

'How did you connect that with Bernard?'

'Randers worked for Bernard sometimes. You must know that,' Magda said. 'I played my editor to send me over on a Bernard story and went to see him at his office. He invited me down here.'

'He invited you, Ball, me and Maria,' I said. 'All of whom had known Randers. Then he played the old tape.'

'But Maria didn't know that,' Alice put in quietly.

Which was very curious indeed, since, at a guess, Bernard had rigged the séance for the purpose of catching the conscience of one of us, yet he had doped out one of the main interested parties.

Not that he could have done much else, I supposed on reflection, since a medium, hearing a tape while fully conscious, would hardly have taken it as anything but a trick.

But if the tape was to have had full effect, why have the séance? Why not have played it straight to the four interested people?

It was Magda who put the thing into some sort of order.

'I begin to wonder whether it is Bernard who is arranging all this,' she said. 'It seems as if he does not know quite enough to get the thing right. Is it possible?'

'Bernard is a frightened man,' said Alice, quietly.

'Why do you say that?' I said.

'By the way his temper goes. Up, down, any old way, taking it out on someone because he cannot reach the one who really is angering him. We have been here before, when he was quite different. That's how I can tell.'

She turned and looked along to the lane.

'Where the hell has Maria gone?' she said, almost angrily. 'I want to get shot of this damn place before it shoots me!'

'I don't want to be depressing,' I said, 'but I'm quite sure that anyone who leaves in a hurry now will have somebody right behind. This isn't a matter of Bernard on his own. The men who killed Ball and cleared up the remains were trained men. There may be a lot of them. I believe that this is a big game we've walked into and the best thing, for the time being, is to pretend ignorance. There really isn't another way, apart from demanding police protection, and you have to give a very sound reason before you get any of that. I don't see a reason here.'

I looked at Alice.

'What do you really know about this business, Alice?' I said.

She looked at the sky as if for advice.

'Maria said she was frightened this time. That's why I came.'

'She hadn't been frightened before?'

'No. Like I said, the first time Bernard was different. Anyhow, that time I came as a van hire for her. I wanted pocket money, that's all. But we got friendly, and this second time she said she wanted me to come because she wasn't sure about things.'

'In what way?'

'She had an idea there was something crooked, that Bernard was out to diddle somebody on a business deal and use the séance to do it with.'

'And that made her nervous?'

'It made her nervous not knowing whether she was right or not.'

'But she did suspect there might be a trick done?'

'That's why she asked me to come the second time.'

'Did she have any reason?'

'You keep overlooking the fact that, whatever your prejudices are, Maria has psychic gifts and she has a very sharp sense of what things may turn out like. She feared this one would turn out to be a mess, and I think she was dead right!'

She looked at me, then at Magda.

'There's three of us here, and we all know there's something really up and that one man's dead already, so what are we going to do about it?' Alice said. 'I suggest, first of all, we find Maria and then think of a way out to where we can all go back where we started from and begin again—in a different direction.'

'Everybody would agree with that,' Magda said. 'It's impossible—'

She broke off and stared past me. I turned my head enough to see to the corner of the lane. A van was coming out of it very slowly. The van was black. It seemed to be an armoured type with dark, wired windows so that we could not see anyone in the front seats. It nosed out of the lane, but did not turn towards us. It seemed to be heading for the slope down to the quarry.

Then it stopped as if a brake had been pulled hard on. And there it stood, blocking the lane and the slope to the quarry.

'What's it doing?' Alice said.

'Sleepwalking,' I said.

'It's one of those security vans, isn't it?' Alice said.

'Only not so secure,' I said. 'The back doors appear to be open.'

Alice began to walk towards it. I followed her.

'Be careful,' I said. 'There's something strange about it.'

'I know. But I've got an idea that Maria—might have met—' She started to run towards the van.

'Hold it!' I said, then ran after her.

I caught her before she reached the back doors of the van and pulled her to one side, away from it.

I held her so she could not do anything but come to a halt. As we stumbled to a standstill the van started to move again and gathered speed as it headed down the slope to the water.

There was no sound but the crunching of the tyres on the hard ground. The whole thing was eerie.

The doors began to flap as the speed increased and we could see inside the body of the thing.

It was then that I realised we were looking in the wrong direction. As the van had moved on it had uncovered the figure of Maria crouching on the ground at the top of the slope. She had her hands clasped to her ears as if scared of being deafened.

The van swung suddenly and crunched against the side of the cutting. There was a tearing of metals and rock and the vehicle came to a slantwise halt across the slope, its front crushed into the rock side.

I let Alice go then and she ran across to the crouching woman.

'Mar! What's happened?'

Alice bent, and as she did Maria turned to her and began to cry like a child.

I looked carefully all round, particularly at the area of the wooded lane, but there was no one but the two women by the top of the slope and Magda, still standing by the caravan.

I went down to the smashed van and opened the driver's door. There was a man inside, lolling towards the far side.

His mouth was open as if he was surprised finding himself dead.

He seemed familiar, and for a moment I could have sworn I had flashed back five years to the time when I had shot Randers dead. He had looked just as surprised as this man did.

It was not Randers. It could not have been Randers, but, for a few awful seconds, it did seem to me that the impossible had happened, and that a man had come to life in order to be shot again.

The likeness was strong between this corpse and Randers. But I had shot Randers in the front of his head; this man had been shot through the back of it.

2

The shock of seeing the dead man's face held me still a second after I should have moved. There was a crunch of metal from somewhere, then I felt the van move against my shoulder.

I jumped back, and the driver's door slammed shut with such a thud that the vibration must have shaken the van free of the last bit of rock it had crushed up against.

The vehicle started to go sideways down the slope, then the front swung round as if straightening up for the last accelerating run into the water.

There was a great burst of spray, and the heavy van went out across the placid lake like a lifeboat being launched down a steep ramp.

It might have floated a little had the rear doors been shut, but as it was, the interior filled up with the great surge of water which followed the splash of the launching, and within three seconds, at most, the vehicle, and the dead man, were sunk out of sight beneath the disturbed surface of the pool.

I turned and tramped back up the slope. The two women were going back towards the caravan, Maria clinging to Alice. Magda was standing watching them and smoking a cigarette.

At the top I looked back at the water, once more still and placid, showing no trace of the murder it had swallowed up.

Alice took Maria into the caravan. A little later, Alice came out alone.

'She's in shock,' Alice said. 'I've given her something. But she told me—what seems to have happened.'

'Seems to have?'

'She's not quite sure about where the van came from. I don't think a lot of questions will help, either. It came up suddenly behind her on the road. She didn't hear it. She thought it must have run on dead leaf mould until it touched the actual metalled surface. There's a lot of leaf mould on the sides of the lane up there.'

'Just tell me what she did say.'

'She went to the lane,' Alice said. 'Nobody was there. She just walked on along it, until it seemed she'd gone far enough and she feared something must have gone wrong.

'She turned round to come back, and then quite suddenly, the van came up from behind her.'

'Meaning to run her down?' I said.

'No. She said it came up alongside, almost as if it had come out of the hedge at the side of the road.'

'Then what?'

'The driver opened the door. She got in. He had a sort of woolly army hat on that was pulled down so she couldn't see much of his face. The doors at the back were open. He drove on very slowly.

'She asked what he was doing and if he had got the message from Bernard. Then she thought there was something funny about his face. She thought she knew him, and she started to say something, but he turned his head away. Then she got suspicious and reached up and pulled the hat off.

'Then she said he fell forward on the wheel. They were coming out of the lane then and she saw the slope down to the water. She told him to stop, but he sort of slopped over and she saw some blood at the back of his head.

'She pulled up the handbrake, opened the

door and jumped out, but the brake couldn't have held properly, and the van went on.

'That's all.' Alice looked at Magda then at me.

'He was shot through the open back doors by a rifle at quite a long range,' I said. 'Probably silenced, as we didn't hear a shot.' I watched her very carefully, and said, '*Did* she see his face?'

'After he'd been shot. When he nearly fell on her. She was hysterical just now. She got it wrong somehow.'

'How?'

'She said it was Randers. That's mad, isn't it?'

'Yes.'

I looked back at the lane.

'You'll have to get her out of here. You're in a worse position than you were before. I can't explain, but there is a faint hope we might keep in touch. Go inside. Make a call on the phone and then cancel it. Give me fifteen seconds.'

'Okay,' she said, and went into the caravan.

I went to my car, blipped the switch for phone interception frequencies, and set the search button. The machine did the rest.

I heard Alice's voice.

'I'm sorry. I've given you the wrong number. I'll have to look it up and ring again.'

'The complete secret agent's radio receiver,' Magda said, looking in at the opposite door.

'Anyone can buy them,' I said, 'given a few pounds.'

'I'll bet.'

Alice came out.

'Now look. I can receive your phone,' I said. 'But you can't ring me so it's a matter of luck whether it's any good at all. Do you understand that?'

'Can you speak to me?'

'Only if you've got the receiver off the hook. Okay?'

'So it's a hit and miss affair?'

'It may be no use at all. Now, take the van back the way you came and turn left into the village. There's a green on the far side, just past the Post Office. Park by the side of that. If you want to contact me, lift the phone and don't call the operator. Just speak the message. I might not be there to hear it, and if something happens and you can't raise me call 999 and start a pan fire.'

'If we have time,' Alice said. 'What about the car?'

'We'll jack it near where you parked before. Keys?' She fetched them. 'I'm sorry to leave you, but we must get back or perhaps nobody will stand any chance of getting away at all.'

'I'll take your word,' Alice said. 'After all, there's nobody else's, is there?'

In a couple of minutes, the parking place almost over-looking the quarry was clear of traffic.

I picked up Magda after she dropped Maria's car by the road verge near the five-bar gate.

'Things seem to be moving,' she said.

'I think they've gone ahead of schedule,' I said. 'The man shot in that van was Randers' double.'

She stared.

'Are you sure?'

'I took a good look. He was very much alike. It shook me at first glance.'

'Oh, then you did know Randers by sight?' she said, curiously.

'Yes.'

'I thought you were just trying to find him. I didn't know you'd met him.'

'Nor did I till afterwards,' I said.

She said nothing.

Bernard was taking sherry, and seemed less on edge than he had done earlier in the day. He was in a good mood for what I had to say, though he must have been severely shaken.

'One of your staff has been playing pranks unsuited to the establishment,' I said.

Bernard looked up sharply. 'How so?'

'Stuck a radio bleeper on my car,' I said, crossly. 'It interfered with the radio. Couldn't find what the matter was so I pulled in at a garage and they found it.'

'It quite spoilt the Mozart, all that bleeping,' said Magda. 'Not that I really like Mozart in the mornings. Too *con spirito*, if that's the term.'

'I'm sorry,' Bernard said. 'But it's more likely to have been a village boy than anyone here.'

We said no more about it.

'Has your guest arrived?' I said.

'Not till this afternoon,' Bernard said.

'Who is it?' Magda said, slyly. 'I must know, darling. Remember my profession, I simply can't not know without bursting my stays, as they say.' She made a kissing motion of the lips. 'A man of *huge* importance, I feel sure, Bernard. Huge. All the world waits on him for the decisions which will make Tomorrow! Tell me!'

'It's just a man called King,' said Bernard. 'And now you're none the wiser, I'm sure.'

Sometimes the brain works as a computer, picking out like and unlike trains from the memory banks. Mine seemed to flash like that as soon as I heard the name.

King, Conqueror, Conquest, King Willow, Pussy Willow, Willow Catkins; Conquest, Catkin, King.

CHAPTER EIGHT

1

'I have heard of many men called King,' said Magda. 'But none of them were kings. What is this one? What does he do?'

'He is a student, one might say. A man of Bonn, the Sorbonne, Oxford, Harvard, Johannesburg—all in various capacities. Undergraduate, graduate, lecturer, professor, exchange professor—every available device known to a man determined never to leave school has been used by Mr King. He has studied politics, history, geology, geography—there are so many, I've forgotten.'

'And he is a close friend?' Magda said, not letting go.

'A friend, and an adviser. After all, he knows so much, Magda. His knowledge can be invaluable to a speculator.'

'What sort of man is he? What does he look like? Is he big? Handsome?'

'He is big. I am no judge of whether he is handsome. He usually tours with an entourage of students. There may be some handsome ones, Magda. I don't know.'

Politics, geography, geology. The subjects registered in my mind, for Charles's work was much affected by these three subjects. He was not interested in the thefts of bullion vans. The mention of robberies had been a connecting link between X and Y, whatever they were, and they had also served to start me off on an investigation which Charles was sure touched Bernard at some point.

I don't think he suspected Bernard, and my experience of his lordship during the last few hours had convinced me that he was right. Bernard was on the edge of his nerves, and that was a bad state for any would-be crook to get into.

Unless, of course, the stakes were so big that an extraordinary tension was almost certain to be set in motion.

I was by then sure that something was storing up in the underground dump, but could not see any connection between stolen bullion, art treasures and something requiring the use of trained squads like the one which had removed the Ball remains.

The events of that morning added to my feeling of suspense over what was going on down there.

The security truck had one item on it which, at the time, I had registered only automatically, having been anxious not to be dragged off into the pool by its sudden decision to run on again from its temporary rest.

The item was the licence disc which had been two years out of date.

The indication there was that it had not been used for two years and further, it might have been one of a series of trucks stolen during the robbery jamboree of some time ago.

Maria had said it had appeared suddenly, and she had not heard it on the metalled lane, and therefore it had come over the soft leaf mulch at the roadside.

In fact, it might have come out of the hedge, because the soft carpet extended either side of the old wire fence.

She had not heard any sounds of the van breaking through a fence such as that so there must have been an opening, even a temporary one, through which it had come.

A few seconds later, the driver had been shot by a sniper standing somewhere behind, probably at the spot where the van had come through the hedge.

So Randers II, as he had appeared to me, had been escaping with the truck. It had been his getaway vehicle. A stolen truck, kept in hiding for two years suddenly snatched and run out through a disguised entrance—which had to be there somewhere—but not quite quickly enough to get ahead of the sniper.

The driver had been dressed in denim overalls, as if he had been a mechanic. Whatever he had been, he had certainly been escaping from the underground, and the occupiers hadn't wanted him to go.

And he had been so *like* Randers . . .

But younger, of course. Randers had been dead five years.

The dead van driver had looked as Randers had looked five years before.

Had there been a younger brother?

All sorts of ideas began to rise in my head, like a younger brother bent on some kind of search for what had happened to Randers I.

The fact that he had clearly been escaping from the underground indicated that he shouldn't have been in there.

Then, in the midst of a desperate escape, when he must have known pursuit was close behind, he had stopped to pick up Maria.

That pause had been his fatal error. If he had kept straight on, accelerating, he would have got beyond the range of the sniper's bullet.

But he had stopped for her, which meant that she had been something more to him than just somebody looking for a lift.

He had known her. He had stopped because of that.

He had known Maria. He had looked like Randers. He might even have sounded like Randers—

My world was full of ideas while that sherry was slowly being sipped.

I had to see Maria that afternoon. At last I had something to see her about.

She might know what was really under the

ground of that wild neglected wood.

*   *   *

King didn't turn up for lunch, but Bernard was much easier in his nerves, as if the coming of King would soon take a great load from his shoulders.

I thought it was because King was Mr Big. A dedicated academic was not the usual class of big-time crook, but crime, like any other subject for study, can become an obsession.

'What time do you expect him?' Magda said, with a brief glance at me before she fastened her eyes on Bernard.

'Any time this afternoon,' Bernard said. 'You know what these academics are. Absent-minded. Things catch their interest and delay them.'

'Of course, yes.' She laughed. 'Eggheads are all the same.'

After lunch I went out on the pretext of getting something from my car. When I got there a ghostly, urgent voice was audible on the radio. I turned it up a little.

'Alice? Blake.'

'She's gone to find the car—'

The voice was interrupted by the operator who thought the line was crossed, but she had to be ignored.

'Why?'

'To come to the house.'

'When did she go?'

'Two minutes.'

'Okay. Leave her. I'll take over.'

The operator was asking questions. I turned off the set altogether, and went back into the house.

'I must get a little exercise before your guest arrives,' I said to Bernard. 'May I borrow a walking stick?'

I borrowed one and set off for the wood before which the caravan had stood on the first occasion I'd seen it. Once out of sight of the house I walked very fast.

I knew the distance from the village green to where Magda had left the car, and hoped I could cover my side of the triangle before Maria covered the distance from the village.

On the way through the wood I caught sight of a figure amongst the trees. It looked like a man standing still, leaning against a tree. It could have been a gamekeeper.

I thought it was one of the underground men, watching me.

There was no point in attracting his physical attention and I walked on as if enjoying a brisk walk, settling my lunch.

I reached the boundary hedge and climbed over. That gave me a chance to look back. The man I had seen had moved nearer to the hedge. There was no doubt in my mind then that he was watching me.

It was unfortunate, but couldn't be helped. I

went to the five-bar gate and got over it. The car was still there on the grass at the side of the road. It was in such a position that trees behind the road hedge prevented it from being seen from Bernard's wood.

The place was quiet but for the birds in and about the trees. I leaned on the gate for a minute or two and consulted a map I had brought from the car. The man was still watching from the wood, though he was being unobtrusive. He may have thought that I had not spotted him and I might not have done had I not been acutely wary.

Looking back at the car I noticed the driver's window was down and wondered if Magda had left it like that.

Then round the curve in the lane I saw Maria coming towards the car. She was walking, unsteadily, I thought, along the grass verge.

I left the gate and walked slowly, and then, when beside the car and the trees, raised my finger to my lips and went towards her. She was looking down, as if thinking hard, and it was a worried, almost tearful sort of thought.

She saw me suddenly and stopped. I went on towards her still keeping my finger raised.

'One of Bernard's men is watching in the wood,' I said quietly.

She hesitated. 'What do you want? What are you doing here?'

'I don't want you to go to Bernard's,' I said.

122

She looked angry.

'Where I go is none of your business!'

'He is expecting a man called King. If you go you might not come out again.'

The warning did not affect her. She frowned as if puzzled.

'King?' she said. 'There was no man called King. Who is he?'

I told her what I knew. She shook her head.

'A learned man. Bernard said, a learned man. One who could work it out. One who could calculate. A man without feeling, but a man of figures and plans—'

She was talking to herself, in a tone she might have used when in a trance, expressionless, asking questions of herself, wondering, finding an answer in step by step of drifting thought.

'Misrer, Mis—Misrule. He used to laugh. Misrule. A name for a king. Yes. King of Misrule. It was part of the plan—'

'Randers' plan?'

She looked up quickly as if she had forgotten I was there and my voice had wakened her with a shock.

'Why are you here?'

'I was here when you were in the van and the driver was shot,' I said. 'I would have got him out, but stood no chance. Anyhow, he was dead. Was that his brother?'

She said nothing.

'Was it Randers' brother?'

'What does it matter? Yes!'

'Be quiet! I told you there is a man in the woods. Randers' brother had got underground and was coming out when you met him.'

She looked at me with fear in her eyes, but her mouth fixed tight shut.

'Maria,' I said gently, 'take the car. Get back to Alice and go away from here. Anywhere. Tell her I said so. You have got yourself into something far too deep for you to get out of. If you go back to Bernard's now you'll be dead, like Randers and his brother. And what could you do, now that the brother's dead? You've got no help—'

'Get in the car,' she said, suddenly and for the first time she took her hands from the pockets of the sloppy linen jacket she wore.

In the right hand she had a small, but probably effective, automatic pistol.

'Oh dear,' I sighed. 'Don't tell me you meant to go to the house and shoot Bernard. What on earth good will that do?'

I got into the car and began to think. She got into the driver's seat. Magda had been told by Alice that the 'hiding place' for the keys was in the disappearing ashtray. Maria got them from there.

I didn't remember any series of events that went wrong as often as this one had.

Maria started up and then shot backwards down the lane. The move was totally unexpected, but it took us right away from the five-bar gate and the watcher beyond it.

She swung across the road and up the grass verge with the intention of making a turn to go forwards along the lane towards the quarry.

I let her do that, but when we came to the end of the lane by the grass where the caravan had parked, I jammed my side hard up against her, pressing her against the door, and switched off the ignition.

We came to an indescribable halt after slewing half round, as if about to go back the way we had come.

'You can't hold someone at gunpoint and drive,' I said holding her tight against the door. 'You should have made me do the driving.'

I got the gun from down by her side, but only after releasing my pressure against her. It was jammed well down against the door.

'You've got to listen to me,' I said. 'This isn't a time for revenge. No matter what you feel about Bernard, leave him alone. He'll hang himself. What you've got to do is get away from here, and that damn quick! Once this man King arrives I wouldn't give a bent match for your life.'

'Leave me alone!'

'To kill yourself? In case you don't know,

there are two men dead already. Ball was murdered last night, in the house.'

She became calmer.

'He had a bad aura. I saw it,' she said.

'What about your own? You should worry more about yourself and less about people who have been dead for years. What good can it do now to get your revenge? You kill Bernard. But Bernard's going to die, anyhow. His card's marked.'

'I marked it!' she said, angry again. 'I did! I don't have to look for signs. I know!'

It would take a long time to quieten Maria down—even if it could be done—and I hadn't the time to try.

'You're crazy, Maria! Why do you want to kill him, anyway?'

'He killed my lover.'

'Who do you mean?'

'The man you call Randers.'

'You're on the wrong line there,' I said. 'Bernard didn't kill him. I know that.'

'But he said he did. He told me! He boasted!'

'Bernard's a liar. He wasn't even there that night.'

She hesitated, uncertain, almost confused.

'How do you know?'

'Because I was there.'

She stared at me in disbelief.

'You? You were there?'

'Yes.'

'Then who shot him? Who did?'

'I did. He came up behind me, but he didn't shoot in time.'

She just sat there staring at me with big eyes. Then she shook her head.

'No. You're saying it to put me off. I know who—'

There was no more time. With regret, I hit her in the back of the neck. She went flaccid. I got out, opened the driver's door and lugged her out on to the grass. I opened the rear door and lifted her in. I left her on the floor, covered in a rug, then got in and drove off back towards the village and the caravan.

When I got there I pulled the car up right by the main caravan door. Alice came out.

'What's happened? You've got her?'

'She's had a knock,' I said. 'Shove her on a bunk and then drive the hell out of here. The whole thing's come to a boil and she damn nearly walked right into it.'

'Go? But you said—'

'You've got to risk it now. Get out as fast as you can.'

We got Maria on to a bed.

'I'll have the car collected and sent back to you one day, when the sun comes out. And just one thing before you go: don't get the police in on this. Maria is not the girl you think she is. Okay? Now beat it!'

As I drove off I saw the van start away and felt some relief. I drove back near to where I had met Maria but left the car out of earshot of the woods; about a quarter-mile downwind.

I strode back, got over the gate and the hedge, then walked fast away through the woods back towards the house. Now and again I saw the shadow of the man who had watched for so long, and seen so little. His interest in me seemed to grow less as I came to the edge of the wood and headed for the house.

The only person I saw as I went in was the all-purpose chauffeur who was sorting some letters in the hall.

'His Lordship is in the library,' he said, and went on sorting letters.

It did not seem that King had arrived.

Bernard was alone in the library, standing staring out of one window as if willing the expected guest to arrive quickly.

He turned as I went into the room and closed the door.

'Had a nice walk?' he said.

'I've been thinking,' I said, and crossed the room to near the window where he stood. I sat on the arm of a chair. 'I've been wondering why in hell you brought Randers into this?'

He thought about it.

'The whole thing was a test,' he said. 'I knew somebody had done business with Randers, and I wanted to know who. I knew it was one of the three of you, but the experiment didn't work.'

'We all knew Randers. We were all in

Germany at the time he was stunting around selling this, that and the other to anyone with an open ear.'

'I said who had done business with him.'

'Isn't that most likely to be Ball?'

'I don't think Ball had the guts.'

'You must have thought he had some, otherwise you wouldn't have had him shot last night.'

He became still as if he had touched a high voltage line so his muscles locked solid.

'You knew that?'

'I saw it.'

His muscles released. He began to pace about, then stopped and looked at me.

'What will you do?'

'What should I do? Ball is not my business. The only thing is, you knew he had been talking to me just before he was shot. Perhaps you shouldn't have shot him until after you'd found out what he told me. That showed a lack of foresight.'

He began to pace again and I watched, just in case he rang any not very obvious alarm bells. But he didn't seem to want to fight this situation. I had judged his nervousness about right—at least, I hoped so.

'He sold me short, Blake. He could have ruined me almost overnight. That was why I couldn't let him go. It was a question of him or me. If he'd won, I would have had to shoot myself. It was that kind of situation he had me in.'

'I can believe you could get yourself so tied up that something might burst, Bernard. There are always dangerous moments in your kind of financing, and I fully understand how you can be taken unawares by sheer bad luck quite suddenly.'

He looked slightly relieved until I put the boot in.

'But Ball didn't tell me about money, Bernard. He didn't mention finance at all.'

Bernard sat down suddenly and held his head in his hands. He said nothing. He hardly moved. He looked like a man genuinely scared to death.

It was at that moment that it began to occur to me that the fact that he was not the Big Chief was not the only reason for his nervousness.

It occurred to me that perhaps he was scared of being found out. It occurred to me that Ball had been shot, not because of what he had told me, but what he was hoping to tell somebody else when he got away. He might have been going to tell somebody what Bernard was really doing, and that once he had done that, Bernard's little number would be up.

'Forget Ball,' I said suddenly. 'I haven't said anything of what he told me. Forget him.'

Bernard looked up incredulously.

'Forget—' he began.

'Go back to where I started,' I said, cutting him short. 'Why did you bring in Randers? Randers died five years ago. Why did you bring him back again?'

'Because I had to know!' He stood up in a sudden rage. 'I had to know what he had done, and who his partner was.'

'But it was five years ago!'

'There's no time limit to hatred, Blake. It can last long after a man is dead, long after you think he's been forgotten.'

'You feared he had a friend who would carry on for him. But after five years, Bernard? Where had this friend been all that time? In prison? Who was the friend? Conquest? Catkin?'

He was shaking as he stood.

'The friend—' he gasped, and for a moment I thought he might collapse.

'You know!' he shouted. 'You know better than anyone who it is! You *know*!'

Then he did collapse. His legs failed and he fell back into the chair gasping.

CHAPTER NINE

1

I loosened his tie and undid his collar. He was making great efforts to pull himself together, but it seemed to me he had something a little more than tension affecting him. He looked as if his heart was not quite equal to the strain.

He sat up and hung his head into his hands. He was trying to control his breathing. He was still in some distress, but I pushed in again before he tried to forget what he had said.

'How do I know who it is, Bernard?' I spoke quite softly, in almost a friendly tone, I thought.

'It failed,' he said. 'The séance failed because the man wasn't here. The one man I should have waited for wasn't here—'

'King,' I said.

He sat back then and stared at me with eyes as big as marbles. Then he closed them and nodded.

'So you're waiting for him and his retinue— to do what? Go in with him again? Or blow his head off?'

'He won't bring anyone,' Bernard said, wearily. 'He's got them here already.'

'The removal squad I saw?'

Again he nodded.

'But five years,' I said. 'What's been happening over the five years since Randers died, that nothing's happened?'

'I don't know. That's why I brought the girl in. She has psychic gifts. Also she was Randers' girl.'

'You wanted Randers back, or something he had?'

'Something he knew.'

'And you only recently found out he knew it? After five years?'

'He was shot in Germany. It was officially put down as a shooting accident. As he was a British traveller, or rep, as they call them, the body was sent back here and buried in a churchyard where somebody claimed his home was. Whether it was ever his home or not, I don't know, but it was where Maria lived, so she was welcome to the remains.'

'So he stayed there five years under the mound and then suddenly somebody remembered him.' I said. 'Why?'

'Because Ball got drunk, and not only drunk but frightened. We all knew Randers had died with a secret, but we had always thought it was in his memory. It was in his head, all right, but that wasn't near enough. He'd got it in a tooth.'

'What?'

'He had the message put in a filling. The dentist must have been in with the idea, but knowing Randers, I'm not sure what happened to him.'

'And he stayed buried with his tooth for five years, and you made a guess who'd got it recently—or at least, the contents. The question remains; why the five years?'

'I don't know.'

'But you knew that the message had come back into circulation?'

'I knew where it had been. And when I heard about the grave—'

'A fair guess. But surely you needed some confirmation? Something else must have happened?'

'I got a phone call from Magda. She said her magazine was interested in getting an interview with me.'

'Why was that suspicious? It's that kind of magazine. Interviews with the powerful, the successful. So why?'

'I remembered that Magda had known Randers. Then Ball was back from a trip. He'd known Randers. Maria—I had used her before, but for trying out market tips—and believe it or not, it worked a couple of times— Maria had been his girl. Then you turned up at my office, and it seemed to me like a full house of Randers admirers.'

'I see, so you wanted to know who'd got the poisoned tooth?'

'I wanted to know who'd got the poison.'

'And it didn't work,' I said.

'It's possible somebody thought the taped

voice was a fake.'

'It's possible that the person you wanted wasn't there.'

He stared at me, and a cunning light began to come back into his eyes as if he was recovering from his series of shocks.

'But everyone who was *in Germany* with him was there. The three who had business with him. King wasn't in Germany.'

'How can you know that was all? There could have been others. Randers was a born cheat.'

'I know the three who were with him at times on the day he was shot.'

'What was the message he had hidden in his fang?'

'I don't know.'

'But you feared it?'

'I feared everything that scoundrel plotted. He would ruin people, force them to suicide even, just for a whim. He hated everybody.'

'He hated himself,' I said. 'That's where the weakness was. Never mind. You called this party to find out who had that message, but it's failed. Failure has shaken you. What do you think was in that message?'

'I don't know.'

'Yet you feared it affected you. But be reasonable. If Randers had a message from himself or anybody else, why hide it where he did? Who was going to look for it there? Granted somebody did in the end, you say, but

135

what sort of message was it that was worth getting after five years? Something five years old is no good to your business, is it? You need up-to-the-minute information, not stuff five years old.

'Five years old and hidden where nobody might ever have found it. Why did he do that? It could only have been that he wanted to carry the message without its being found. It's possible he didn't even know what was in it, because as you know, there are ways of finding out what a man knows; specially a two-faced villain like Randers. So it's most likely he didn't know, and that he agreed to the dental work for money alone. In fact he was paid to be the carrier and for nothing else. So the only thing that he might have told about the secret message is who the man was who gave it and paid him.'

'Randers must have known what it was. He made it his business to know everybody else's.'

'All right. Whether he did or not does not alter the main fact that a secret message carried then could have little importance now. Things change too much in politics. So it really goes back to your original fear; that it had something to do with revenge.

'But, Bernard, why is that so important now when it's perfectly clear that you have something up your sleeve with this man King that you clearly hope will make both your fortunes even bigger than yours is now.'

'Mine isn't big now,' Bernard said suddenly. 'Somebody has been playing against me, and it's beginning to be unpleasant.'

'Do you know who it is?'

'It might be a consortium. I don't know.'

'Even if you lose on paper, you've got cashables to fall back on, Bernard. I'm sure you'll have thought of that, in case anything went wrong. What business is King in?'

He looked at me with a hard brilliance in his eyes that made me think, for a moment, that he might be near to madness.

'Death!' he said, savagely. 'That's his business! Death!'

2

He got out of the chair and stood so rigidly he began to tremble from the strain.

'Funny that,' I said. 'I thought you were looking forward to seeing him.'

He laughed shortly.

'I'd look forward to seeing him with his throat cut. And he knows it. That's the trouble. Sometimes I think it will be a race to see which of us gets there first.'

'Why should he kill you? You're a partner.'

'On the contrary, I'm the mug,' Bernard said. 'I do what he says. That's the position, Jonathan.'

'Blackmail?' I said.

'Worse. Sheer brute force, and I'm the fool

who allowed it to be built up all round me till I'm a prisoner in a scheme I wish I'd never heard of.'

'You must have expected to make something out of it.'

'The original idea, yes. But that was just a cover for what's been built up after.'

'What?' I said. 'What's been built?'

Magda came in. The spell was broken. Bernard regained some of his usual calm as he turned to her.

'Where is this man of yours?' Magda said.

'He will come,' said Bernard.

'You sound like doom,' said Magda.

'Possibly,' said Bernard, and smiled without humour.

'Where has Ball flown to?' Magda said. 'Is it back to Arabia?'

'Somewhere there,' said Bernard. 'He's all over the place.'

'To me he seems too miserable to sell anything,' Magda said, and shrugged. 'But what matters is if they trust you, even though you look like the end of the world.'

She still had on the suit she had worn with me that morning, but she was carrying a satchel bag slung over her shoulder which was a different colour from the one she had taken in the morning. It did not match her shoes as the morning one had done.

I wish I had guessed then at the reason for the change but I don't really think the hidden intention was guessable.

She was in the same, cheerful, rather teasing mood she had been in through lunch, as if she found it amusing to needle Bernard about his visitor.

Obviously she didn't know the facts about Bernard and his visitor as he had explained them to me. And I believed him, and I had the feeling that if she heard it, she would, too.

The chauffeur-general knocked and looked in almost in one continuous action.

'In about ten minutes, sir,' he said.

Bernard nodded and the man went out again.

The message seemed to me to indicate that in ten minutes King would arrive, though I would have been interested to know how the chauffeur had known that. Unless King, also, had had a bleeper stuck on his approaching car, and the chauffeur was plotting its course.

Bernard went into a brown study just after the news, and his eyes were constantly drifting towards the windows and the drive outside.

Magda sat on the arm of a chair, took a mirror out of the satchel bag and surveyed her make-up. She was not satisfied and took out a lipstick and began to use it while concentrating on the effect in the mirror.

Perhaps she was making herself presentable for the oncoming King.

'I take it this isn't a private meeting you're expecting?' I said.

'Certainly not!' Bernard said. 'You may talk him out of his senses if you like.'

The opportunity for that was not to come, as it turned out.

'Why do you have people you don't like?' asked Magda, putting her repair outfit back in the bag.

'In business, one can't avoid it. You know that.'

I looked out beyond the drive and the trees which screened the house from the road, a quarter of a mile away. To the right there was a break in the trees, and I could see a part of a vehicle which appeared to be parked just by the trees on the house side of the road.

Only a part of the vehicle showed, but I felt sure I recognised it as Alice's caravan.

I felt a wave of uneasiness as I saw it. So Maria had had her own way and they had come back into the danger area.

But why had they stopped out there, getting on for half a mile from the house gates? Had courage failed so close? But I could not imagine Maria or Alice suddenly losing courage, no matter what the distance. If they had stopped short, it was for a reason, and between them, I believed, they could cook up a good, strong one.

A car appeared on the drive, a Rolls-Royce of rather dusty appearance.

'Is this the man?' I said, turning.

Bernard hurried to the window and

stared—almost glared—out.

'That's it,' he said, turning away. 'You'd think he could afford a carwash.'

Bernard's mind was obviously dodging the main thoughts in his head, coming out with an aside like that.

'Let's go and meet the man,' said Magda, getting up. 'I am agog.'

Bernard gestured towards the door. She went smartly ahead, smiling at him as she passed. There was a kind of chic insolence about her then, almost as if showing him that she, and not he, would be the most important person at the meeting.

Which was damned right.

She went out. I followed and Bernard came last. We came into the hall and saw the Rolls sweep round on the gravel and stop by the house steps. It seemed that one fat man and four slim young men got out of the car.

Magda was directly facing the door, I stood on her right and Bernard, still glaring, on her left. The chauffeur-domo went and opened the glass-paned door as the fat man came up the steps, the four men forming a square behind him.

The fat man came in smiling, but shading his eyes a little with one hand to accustom himself to the shade after the bright sunlight outside.

As if in a slow-motion dream, I saw Magda flip back the flap of the satchel bag and take out of its capacious maw a .45 automatic which seemed grotesquely out of place in her small, manicured hand.

That hand did not shake except from the recoils as she depressed the trigger and fired four shots into the fat body of the man.

It was like seeing a balloon punctured and flop about, uncertain which way physics would force it to go. First the man staggered back a pace, then half turned, gasped, put his hands up towards his head and then the whole body collapsed and rolled over on the mat, pouring blood.

A .45 makes big holes.

Magda put the gun back in the bag and turned to me with a half smile.

'I shall be in my room,' she said. 'I have a slight headache.'

She walked away up the stairs.

Bernard went two paces towards the obviously dead body, then turned, came and took my arm. He muttered a terrified oath, and I thought for a moment he was holding me to save himself from falling, but he recovered and urged me towards the library we had just left.

As we went I saw the four young men gather round their fallen leader as if wondering what to do about it, and then bend over him.

We got into the library. Bernard let go my arm and put his hands to his face.

'He's dead! In Heaven's name, what now?'

'What now, Bernard? But surely it's what you wanted, isn't it?'

He dropped his hands and shook his head, his eyes shut as if he was crying.

'Why in hell did she do it?' he whispered. 'How can I manage?'

The question shook me as much as the whole incident had. I had seen many shootings in the course of my business, but never one quite so cold, calm and unexpected as that Magda had just performed.

'Who is that man?' I said, grabbing Bernard's arm tightly. 'Who is he?'

'King was several people. He was a promoter, entrepreneur, always plenty of money to back shows and—other things—'

'Like robbery?'

'Perhaps. He was Maria's promoter when she did shows in Brussels. But they weren't séances then. They were strip shows. That kind of thing. I think he called himself Grimalkin then. He called himself many things in the course of his career.'

'Now he's dead. Why can't you manage without him?'

'But I don't bloody well know enough! I don't know exactly what he worked up. He told me only what I had to know. The rest of it was known only to himself. He didn't trust anybody. I wonder, now he's dead, if he trusted *anyone* enough to tell them the whole thing, otherwise what in hell will happen?'

'There must be records, notes. Something of that sort.'

'There might be. Knowing him, I doubt it. He could memorise. And further—'

A sudden movement at one of the windows made me turn. I saw the dusty Rolls swing round on the drive and head down it towards the gates and away. I could see quite clearly that it contained just the four young men who had formed the pre-funeral entourage.

I went to the door and out along to the hall. The chauffeur-domo was pushing a vacuum cleaner away from the main door towards a cupboard.

There was no sign that Grimalkin, or King, or Catkin, or Conquest had ever been there, let alone bled there.

The chauffeur glanced briefly at me as he shoved the cleaner into the cupboard. He closed the door, stood to attention for a moment, as if letting the wrinkles fall out of the sleeves of his natty uniform, then he reached into the cupboard, brought out a clothes-brush and proceeded to disperse the faintest trace of dust.

Anyone would think that clearing up after murders was a customary exercise in this peculiar household.

I went up the broad stairs and along the corridor to the door of Magda's room. I knocked. It struck me as humorous, that polite deference of knocking indicating a quiet desire to go in and query the reasons of a murderess, without inconveniencing her.

'Come in.'

I went in. She was in the business of changing and wore a very brief pair of black knickers.

'So,' she said, putting her suit jacket on a hanger, 'you want to know why I blew his bloody bull head off?'

'Roughly that, yes.'

'It is plain curiosity?' She looked at me for a moment, then carried the jacket and put it carefully in a wardrobe trunk.

'Do you always travel with a bloody great thing like that?'

She looked at the standing trunk.

'It belonged to my grandmother,' she said. 'I am fond of it.'

'It can carry a lot of changes.'

'It has to. I leave it in London for when I come.'

'Okay. So why did you blow his bloody bull head off?'

'It was a matter of social conscience,' she said, and began putting on a bra.

'Saving the world as we know it?'

She laughed.

'Part of it. *Part* of it.'

'Just that part which affects you?'

'You are a cynical man.' She took up a skirt and stepped into it. She was shifting it into position round her waist when she added, 'Do you know who he really was?'

'I know four names, but none means anything to me.'

There was a knock at the door and then an almost instantaneous opening that I had seen before. The chauffeur looked in.

'Tea is in the library,' he said. 'His Lordship begs to be excused.'

'We need only music,' I said, 'to make this a comic opera.'

'Not for you, sir,' I heard the chauffeur say, but it was so softly said that without sharp hearing I would never have heard it at all.

CHAPTER TEN

1

Magda came and kissed me, then patted my cheek.

'He was warning you, darling,' she said.

'He is a portable warning,' I said. 'He needs no talk. To get back to saving the world as we know it. You didn't approve of what King had in mind?'

'I didn't approve of King.'

'Right. He was carrying the thing too far, you thought?'

She cocked her head and looked curiously at me.

'What do you know about it all, Jonathan?'

'Let's start with the old, dead, mutual friend, Randers, and make up a story around him. First, he was a greedy man. He never sold anything once. He sold it to both sides at once and got double the money. Sometimes he came across old papers in his Continental searches. He found such a one in Berlin. Old Luftwaffe files about targets in this country, including ammunition dumps. In the course of his normal spying duties he found out over here that the details of one special dump— among several—had been lost to the Ministry during its return to London offices. A case of mislaid files used for lighting the office fire perhaps.

'This one dump was on an estate owned by a man killed in the war and passed to a sister who lived in the house and gradually let everything go down and down from lack of interest. Then Bernard bought it from her.

'Now this cost an awful lot of money, and Bernard isn't a country sort of man, but he came with a collection of art stuff bought to furnish the house with. Very soon the place was burgled and the wife murdered. Nothing was ever recovered. Nor is any amount of stuff stolen in burglaries, robberies and hi-jackings. Everything disappeared. Nothing ever came on to the criminal market. Somebody was building up a fortune. Something like Aladdin's Cave was being built up. But what for? Do you know, Magda?'

'There are always crackpots,' she said. 'The more you can afford, the more cracked you can be. And you think the dump is here, on the estate?' she added.

'Of course. So do you. That's why you shot King. Until then he'd been the boss of this enterprise. That's why you shot Ball, too. He had found what you were up to and he went in order—not to fly to Arabia and get lost—but to warn King and so keep himself from getting lost.'

She sat beside me on the bed.

'It does not occur to you that I am saving

148

people from something very unpleasant?'

'Such as what? Was King enlisting a private army of crooks to rob so widely that the economy would be ruptured?'

'You know, once an economy is overturned a very dangerous situation appears. And do you know it can be overturned just by flooding the country with first-class forged banknotes? It's that easy. But if you have a system of taking all the things of intrinsic value, so that you're the only one with real wealth, you're the next Croesus.'

'To do that you'd need to recruit an army of robbers, as I said. A private army. Is that what King was after?'

'He had illusions of grandeur. I don't believe it ever could have come off,' Magda said. 'But if he'd been frustrated just when he believed it was going to work, an awful lot of people would have been killed by his private criminal army.'

'And that's what you were saving us all from?' I said.

'You are a cynical bastard,' she said.

'I just want to be satisfied that you didn't kill them so that you could take the valuable collection that exists so far?' I said, and got up.

'What would it matter to you if that's the case?' she said.

'No one is safe while in possession of ill-gotten gains,' I said.

'Oh, you're thinking of my safety?'

'I'm always thinking about safety. Shouldn't we go down to tea?'

She got up.

'It was so interesting to talk, I had forgotten the invitation. I'll be down.'

I went down to Bernard. He seemed to have been talking to the chauffeur who left the room immediately I went in.

'What are you going to do?' Bernard said.

'Do about what?' I said.

'Dammit, man! Murder!'

I sat down by the small tea table.

'But there's no mystery, is there? We know who did it. May I pour some tea?' I did.

I looked past him to the end window. The caravan had gone, it seemed. There were two heavy lorries going by, and three cars, obviously held up by the juggernauts, followed behind, fidgeting to get by.

I wondered why the girls had brought the van almost to the house, but felt relieved they had gone again.

'What are you going to do, Bernard?' I said. 'The murder was on your carpet.'

'Police you mean? I've done nothing. I wanted to talk to you first.'

'You are not in any position to call the police over King's death?'

He hesitated, then agreed. 'No.'

'Just how far did you mean to go into this robbery racket at the start?'

He shrugged.

'It was just greed. It looked good. I should have to do very little. Just buy this place and then sit back and watch the profits come in. But that was some time ago. Things changed once King realised how easy it was and how powerful it could make him. He started playing around with ideas of revolutions, takeovers of the bloody country—and maybe he could have done it up to the point of a civil-war situation with his own private army and gangs of rioters, looters, arsonists and Lord knows who else. He'd gone beyond the idea of just cleaning up—'

'How did you meet Maria?' I said.

He was startled by the question. 'Eh? Maria! Oh Ball found her.'

'And she'd known Randers,' I said. 'Which made it cosy.'

'I never mentioned Randers to her until this visit.'

'She was his girl friend and King's protégée. King was her manager. Why on earth did you think she would be a straight medium with all those connections?'

'I did not know of all those connections at the beginning,' Bernard said. 'This last year, for me, has been a period of finding out, painfully, how well I've been taken for a mug.'

'I did not know you were a master of self-pity. Your office staff would be surprised.' I poured more tea.

Magda came in.

151

'Come, have tea,' I said. 'As you have saved the world, take a cucumber sandwich to boot.'

She smiled and sat down.

'Do you get paid for shooting the fat man?' I said, and offered the dish of sandwiches.

'Paid? Who by?' She sounded angry.

'Well, Bernard.'

'But Bernard was there. He didn't have to pay anybody. He could have done it!' She laughed.

'So you really did do it for love of the world and its suffering millions,' I said. 'When did you find out Randers had a brother?'

She hesitated then and covered the pause by biting a sandwich.

'Don't worry about giving him away,' I said. 'he's dead.'

She stared at me.

'It was a few months ago,' she said. 'He came to the office to sell a story about his brother.'

'Where had he been for five years? Did he tell you?'

'Prison. East Germany. He had been there with his brother on some business—whatever that was. He was arrested; his brother got away.'

'So the brother knew about the tooth?'

'Oh yes. That was the story he came to me with.'

'And you kept it to yourself.'

'Naturally. I'd known Randers, you see. And

152

I realised that if he'd been to that trouble, the message in his tooth was worth having.'

'Then the brother did the exhumation?'

'Oh yes. Like his brother, he was not a fussy man. He did not mind what he did so long as it was profitable in the end.'

'What was the message?' Bernard said. They were the first words he had uttered since she had entered the room.

'There was no such tooth in the bony remains,' said Magda, with fine feeling. 'It had been taken before he had been buried.'

'So one other person had known about it, besides the brother,' I said.

'The message must have been about the underground dump,' Bernard said. 'What else? What else?'

'Would anyone go to that trouble for something that might be found in a missing file at a Government office? It isn't a small affair. It's several acres of underground works.'

'But forgotten. Written off donkey's years ago!' Bernard snapped. 'There's no mention on the house deeds or any other papers to do with the estate. It was written off years ago!'

'Suppose Randers found out about it, and then came to see it for himself,' I said. 'And then, what he found was interred in his tooth. So it must have been something more than the dump itself. Something he found while he was down there. Something immovable, or he, being Randers, would have pinched it.'

Magda laughed shortly.

'You seem to know what he was but not what he did,' she said.

I looked at the windows.

'Should we not think of what King may do?'

'Do?' said Magda, sharply. 'But he's dead!'

'But his friends aren't,' I said. 'How many men are in the underground, Bernard?'

'Six, I think.'

'Then where's the secret army?'

'If I knew that I'd have been able to sleep nights,' Bernard said. 'But I told you, he'd left me out in the cold. All I knew was what happened here. What he planned away from here he kept to himself, always promising to let me into it when he'd got it right, as he said.'

'Then who's his second?' I said quickly.

'I don't know of any. Certainly not me.'

'He must have had a lieutenant.' I got up and went to the window to look out, then turned round. 'You may have cut off Hydra's head, Magda. Did you think of that?'

She shrugged.

'We shall see, obviously,' she said.

The chauffeur came in from behind her with a silver pot of fresh tea under a white napkin. He put it down and then stepped back.

I thought it curious he hadn't taken the old pot, but had left both together on the tray. At that moment I saw his hand move under the napkin.

There was a table by my hand and a heavy

154

glass ashtray on it. I swept it off in my hand and lobbed it—there was no time for any other sort of throw—at his head. It hit him on the cheek as he saw it coming and half turned his head away to avoid it.

I ran, jumped on an intervening chair seat, sprang off the cushion and down on the other side fairly close to him. He turned towards me, the knife in his hand meant for Magda now turned towards me. I swerved to go round him and he turned with me, striking at me with the knife so well it ripped my left sleeve right down for almost a foot. As he drew the knife back I grabbed his other wrist and put my right foot against his left. That gave me leverage and I spun him off his feet and head first against the wall. He had a solid bone head and despite the crash on it, he slithered round and flung himself at my legs. I sidestepped and he scrambled up to his knees with the knife still in his hand. He made a good try for my arm with it and got to his feet at the same time, but his back was bent forward and he was off balance when I hit him at the side of the jaw and banged him against the arm of Magda's chair. She was then kneeling on it, looking down at his rather dazed face as he crashed, and pointing her big forty-five right into his eyes.

Despite his shaken condition, he recognised what it was, and probably he remembered how expertly she could use it. He just sat back on his heels and waved his hands as if to suggest he understood her.

'He was about to stick a knife in your neck,' I said, picking the weapon up from the carpet. 'The back, of course.'

Bernard was on his feet, glaring at his man.

'What the hell are you playing at?' he shouted.

'It doesn't matter to you,' the chauffeur said. 'You won't last long enough. If I'd done this, you'd have stood a chance, but not now.'

2

'You come with me,' I said, and heaved the chauffeur up by the neck of his jacket.

He went ahead of me to the door, stood aside for me to open it, then went out just ahead. I followed closely. He was so well behaved because until the door fell to behind me, Magda had been pointing the forty-five at him. Once outside his manner changed, but only for a moment. He turned to me as if to say something and then noticed that I had my thirty-eight in my hand.

'You wanted to say something?' I said.

'No,' he said, and became obedient again. He had good cause to believe that any gun in this house was as likely to be fired with intent as not.

'Take me down to the cellars,' I said.

He stopped but did not turn round to me.

'It'll be rough,' he said.

'You'll be in front of me,' I said.

He stayed still a moment, then walked on towards the games room.

We went the way I had found before. In the wine cellar he told me there was a torch on a shelf. I told him to get it and he brought it to me. I took it.

'Which side are you on?' I asked him.

He considered the matter.

'It's suicide, but I'll stick to the noble lord,' he said. 'I've been with him for a long time. Seen him come down on his dignity. The man King is all right dead, but he's got too many behind him. They'll kick.'

'He's got them here?'

'No. Place called Paddock's End. Was a stables. Training. Over towards the Downs. About thirty miles. I think it'll be a bad party once that lot gets loose. King held them under. He held everybody under.'

'Let's get on,' I said.

We went on to the door where I had been almost collared, and he hesitated there.

'There are six men the other side,' he said. 'Armed.'

'Okay,' I said. 'Just don't make a noise with the lock.'

I held the torch while he unlocked the door then stood back.

'There's lights the other side,' he said.

'Good,' I said. 'Show me.'

'You want me to go ahead,' he said.

'I wouldn't trust you behind. But for the time being, I'm on your side till you make a wrong move. Then I'll shoot you with the others.'

'You've only got six shots.'

'That's enough. I'll break your neck.'

His frozen face broke for a moment. He almost grinned, then turned back to the door.

The gun was ready in my hand. My nerves were on edge, listening for the din of an alarm bell when the door was opened. But there was silence.

There is something about absolute quiet which is unnerving. Even the chauffeur stopped breathing, as if to listen better as he opened the door to the incredible stillness.

'What's the matter?' I whispered in his ear.

'Something's wrong,' he said so quietly I hardly heard it.

The lights were on. We looked down an enormous cave, its roof strutted up by soldier-like lines of columns. There were two lorries and a light van scattered about, almost lost in the squat vastness of the cavern. There was no sound anywhere.

'No alarm, no guard,' the chauffeur whispered. 'What the hell's happened?'

I saw a heap covered by sacks lying against a wall alongside our door. There was a foot sticking out from under the sacks.

'Go over there,' I said. 'Lift up the sacks.'

He did as he was told and uncovered eight

dead men. There was Ball and King, then six other men, all in blue overalls, just piled down beside them.

The bodies of Ball and King were the victims of revolver shots; the other six had been machine-gunned and it was a mess.

'There's a room there they used,' the chauffeur said.

He pointed to a set of offices made by metal office partitions. When we looked in, one was a pretty well-stocked armoury, with hand-guns and rifles, Brens and grenades. A lot of it was old but all of it looked efficient and well maintained.

'Yet they didn't shoot back,' I said. 'They seem to have been shot standing against the wall where they fell.'

We went on. There were other rooms, one used as a mess, sleeping quarters with bunks; then there was a lavatory, a bathroom and a phone on a desk in the end room. I used it. I told Charles about the disused stables.

'That's up to you, but you may be too late,' I ended.

We went out into the great cave again. We went and looked in the nearest lorry. It was empty. We could see from a distance that the second lorry was also empty.

So where was Aladdin's Cave?

Doubts began to crawl into my mind. Certainly there were the remnants of a small body of trained men lying against the wall in this place, but that was all there was of the whole story of untold wealth and power beneath the wood.

Perhaps there were more men in the old stables; I knew of the four who had come with King, but that was all.

And the booty of the years, for which this dump had been brought out of the forgotten world to house, just wasn't there.

'Is there anything missing?' I said.

'A lot,' the chauffeur said. 'A lot of crates and stuff was stacked over in the far corner. Army surplus.'

'Are you sure it was that?'

'The boxes were regulation marked.'

As I stood in the silent place I thought again of the matter of the Randers tooth; the secret which seemed to have gone to him during his visit to the dump.

What could it be? I thought of the environment in which the dump stood, and the disused quarry, which must have been in use years after the war had finished, or much more vegetation would have grown around it. Left alone, vegetation gets around. Ask a gardener about his weeds.

I walked down towards the end of the cavern. The chauffeur, by then used to the discipline of my revolver, came with me.

The end of the cavern was a place of concrete-lined bays and nooks. Beyond the end wall, not very far off, would be the limit of the quarry diggings. A dig through from the quarry to the cavern would have been dead easy, given all the tools and machinery lying around in quarry workings.

But people had been using the place for months. They would have found any such connection.

Yet Randers had had a tooth—

We walked on and around the corner from where we stood was a wide ramp going up a wagonway out of the place and into the camouflage of the wood.

There were dirt-mould tracks there which at first looked like old stains of damp coming down the concrete surface. It was only when I went to go up the slope I saw what the tracks really were.

'Let's get back,' I said.

He turned without a word and went ahead.

Sometimes an idea gets into one's head and stays in the background where it exercises a silent influence on succeeding ideas. All along I had been influenced by Randers, mainly because he had been a link connecting each of the four people in the house. I had been influenced by what people he had known and where they had met in Germany five years ago.

What I had not considered was that one of the strongest links made at that time and in that country was not Randers and anybody else, but Randers' girl friend and a woman who could pay for good stories.

161

Those two women had been in the house during my visit here, but the thought of the Randers connection had overlaid that fact in my mind.

Whether it was private armies and secret places to house them, or the plain organisation of a world-wide thieving bureau, the getting of it all together must have taken years. It had had to start as an idea, then be worked up, then be used as a basis for a wide survey of physical and financial possibilities, and the life of such a conspiracy could well have extended back beyond the time that Randers had ceased to be.

He had found the secret dump; the premises for the great world-wide operation. And then he must have sold the idea to someone.

The secret in his tooth was not anything to do with the dump, but was the name of the person to whom he had sold the idea.

King had used it; so had Bernard, but neither was the buyer of Randers' idea. The very name Catkin, which Charles had felt was very nearly the right one, was not a sort of name a man would choose. Catkin, Pussy Willow, both have a feminine aura.

The body had been buried by Maria's English home and the tooth had been taken then.

Randers' brother had not been shot that morning because he was escaping from the

162

dump but because he knew the name on the tooth. Maria had not been wandering aimlessly up the lane but had deliberately gone to a spot where she could stop the van and from which a safe shot could have been fired into the driver's back.

The caravan had been waiting outside the house that afternoon quite openly because the girls were no longer fearful of being seen from the house.

They knew there was no more danger from the trained squad from the underground place, because they knew they were all dead.

The shot in the back of the van, then, had probably been fired by Bernard himself, and the squad were then killed by a 'friend' they recognised.

The killing of King had also been an arranged affair, and the necessity of sharp-shooting in the morning, and then waiting the hours for King to arrive, had shown up in the state of Bernard's nerves.

'I think we'd better hurry,' I said.

But hurrying was no good. The house was empty when we got back into it. Bernard and Magda had skipped together, probably with the girls in the caravan, and they were now on their way following a couple of load-carrying lorries on their way to goodness knew where. Perhaps another forgotten dug-out in the country.

I was about to phone the police with the

number of the caravan in the lost hope that the ladies might be found in it, when three cars and a truck swung into the drive and made noisy halts out on the gravel. At least twenty men leapt out and came running towards the house, displaying arms of various kinds.

I think I sighed and looked at my captive.

'It's the stable lads, sir,' he said, and shrugged.

We were in the library then and heard the men rushing into the house with unnerving clarity. It sounded like hundreds and it came past our door like a stampede of cattle. The door was flung open. My gun was then in my pocket. It is no use being heroic when faced with automatic weaponry in the hands of twenty men.

Only one man came in, but with a large Luger in his hand. He pointed it at us as we stood by the phone.

'Hold it there!'

He took up station by the door, watching us and listening to the others as they entered the games room and obviously prepared an assault on the caverns below. The noise faded into the cellars.

'You're a little late,' I said.

The gunman shrugged.

'Late for what?' he said.

'Everything's gone. The place is empty.'

'We'll find that out for oursleves.'

It seemed that minutes ticked by in an

unsociable silence and then, out of the blue and golden afternoon, came an earthquake.

There was a deep, uneasy roaring as if from many miles away. The windows rattled violently, the floor shook. The gunman looked at the ceiling as the roaring seemed to go on— and on.

I had heard that in wartime, when valuable situations might be in danger of capture by invaders, paratroops and other villains, these places were wired up for total destruction.

The system had waited for more than forty years, but it had destroyed some invaders at last.

As our guard turned to look into the shaking passage to find out what was happening I went up behind him and stuck my gun in the small of his back.

I have wondered since if Randers had known about the old destruct system which had clearly been forgotten, together with the structure it was protecting, and felt lucky we hadn't tripped it as the private army had.

*   *   *

Bernard later turned up in a police station, claiming he had been kidnapped and held prisoner. It seemed he preferred to face the law to staying with the three witches, even with all their booty.

Charles is now looking for them—at least,

he organises the search. So far they haven't been found, but, sooner or later, they will have to start selling something from Aladdin's Cave and then Charles will smile at last.

We hope you have enjoyed this Large Print book. Other Chivers Press or G.K. Hall & Co. Large Print books are available at your library or directly from the publishers.

For more information about current and forthcoming titles, please call or write, without obligation, to:

Chivers Press Limited
Windsor Bridge Road
Bath BA2 3AX
England
Tel. (01225) 335336

OR

G.K. Hall & Co.
P.O. Box 159
Thorndike, Maine 04986
USA
Tel. (800) 223-2336

All our Large Print titles are designed for easy reading, and all our books are made to last.